W9-AXN-476

BASED ON THE ORIGINAL CHARACTERS CREATED BY

JiM DAViS

NEW YORK

GRAPHIC NOVEL #1
"FISH TO FRY"

GRAPHIC NOVEL #2
"THE CURSE OF
THE CAT PEOPLE"

COMING SOON:

GRAPHIC NOVEL #3
"CATZILLA"

GRAPHIC NOVEL #4
"CAROLING CAPERS"

GARFIELD & Co GRAPHIC NOVELS ARE AVAILABLE IN HARDCOV-
ER ONLY FOR $7.99 EACH. PLEASE ADD $4.00 FOR POSTAGE
AND HANDLING FOR THE FIRST BOOK, ADD $1.00 FOR EACH
ADDITIONAL BOOK.

PLEASE MAKE CHECK PAYABLE TO:
NBM PUBLISHING

SEND TO:
PAPERCUTZ, 1200 COUNTY RD. RTE. 523
FLEMINGTON, NJ 08822 (1-800-886-1223)

WWW.PAPERCUTZ.COM

"GARFIELD TV SERIES" © 2008- DARGAUD MEDIA BASED
UPON "THE GARFIELD SHOW" ANIMATED TV SERIES, DEVEL-
OPED FOR TELEVISION BY PHILIPPE VIDAL, ROBERT REA AND
STEVE BALISSAT, ADAPTED FROM THE COMIC STRIP BY JIM
DAVIS. A DARGAUD-MEDIA AND FRANCE 3 COPRODUCTION.
ORIGINAL STORIES BY JULIEN MAGNAT (CURSE OF THE CAT
PEOPLE), MATHILDE MARANINCHI & ANTONIN POIRÉE (THE PET
SHOW), CHRISTOPHE POUJOL (BONE DIGGERS). © DARGAUD
2010 WWW.DARGAUD.COM WWW.THEGARFIELDSHOW.COM

JANICE CHIANG — LETTERING
ADAM GRANO — PRODUCTION
MICHAEL PETRANEK — ASSOCIATE EDITOR
JIM SALICRUP
EDITOR-IN-CHIEF

ISBN: 978-1-59707-267-0

PRINTED IN CHINA
FEBRUARY 2011 BY O.G. PRINTING PRODUCTIONS, LTD.
UNITS 2 & 3, 5/F, LEMMI CENTRE
50 HOI YUEN ROAD
KWON TONG, KOWLOON

DISTRIBUTED BY MACMILLAN
FIRST PAPERCUTZ PRINTING

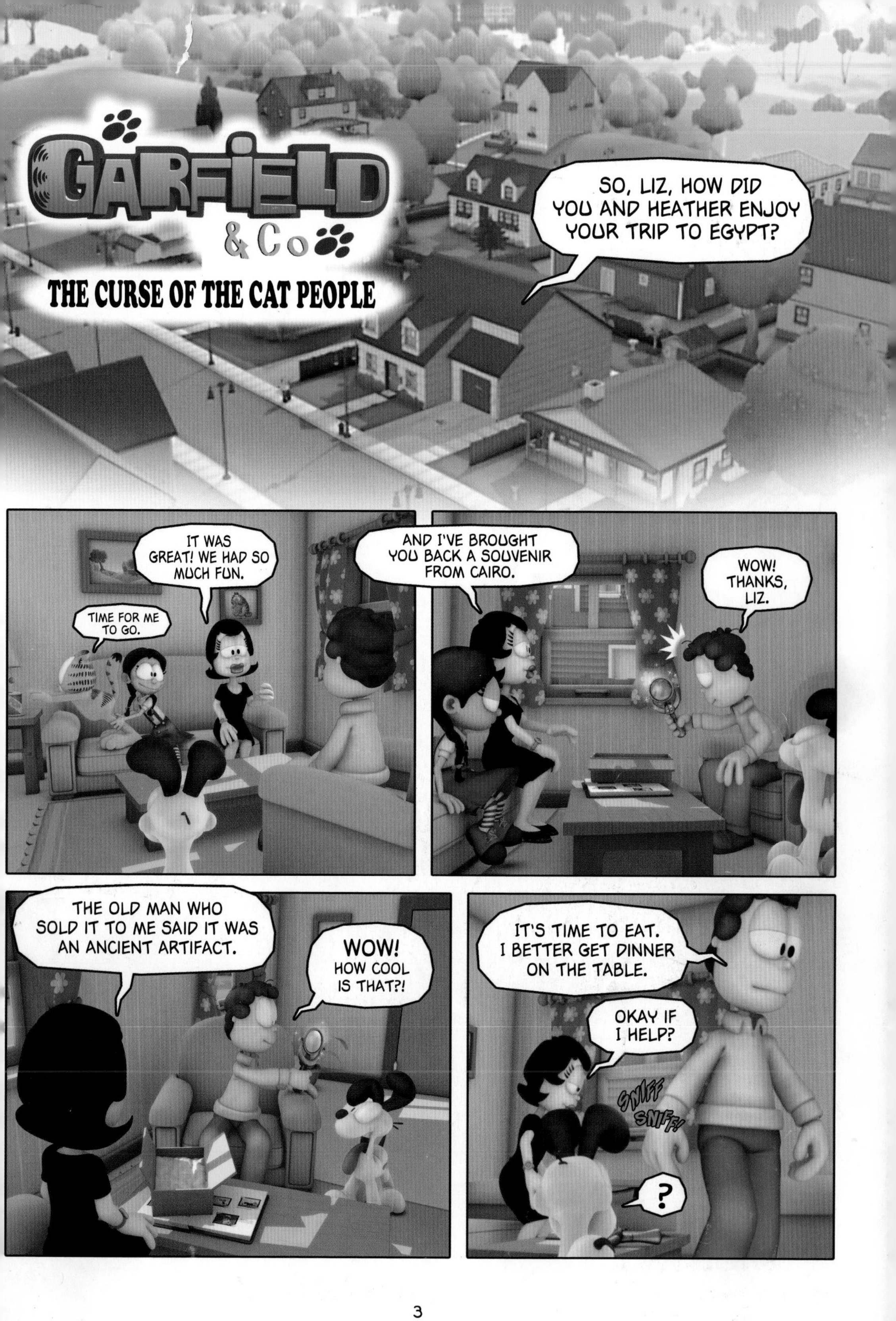
GARFIELD & Co
THE CURSE OF THE CAT PEOPLE
SO, LIZ, HOW DID YOU AND HEATHER ENJOY YOUR TRIP TO EGYPT?
IT WAS GREAT! WE HAD SO MUCH FUN.
TIME FOR ME TO GO.
AND I'VE BROUGHT YOU BACK A SOUVENIR FROM CAIRO.
WOW! THANKS, LIZ.
THE OLD MAN WHO SOLD IT TO ME SAID IT WAS AN ANCIENT ARTIFACT.
WOW! HOW COOL IS THAT?!
IT'S TIME TO EAT. I BETTER GET DINNER ON THE TABLE.
OKAY IF I HELP?
SNIFF
SNIFF!
?

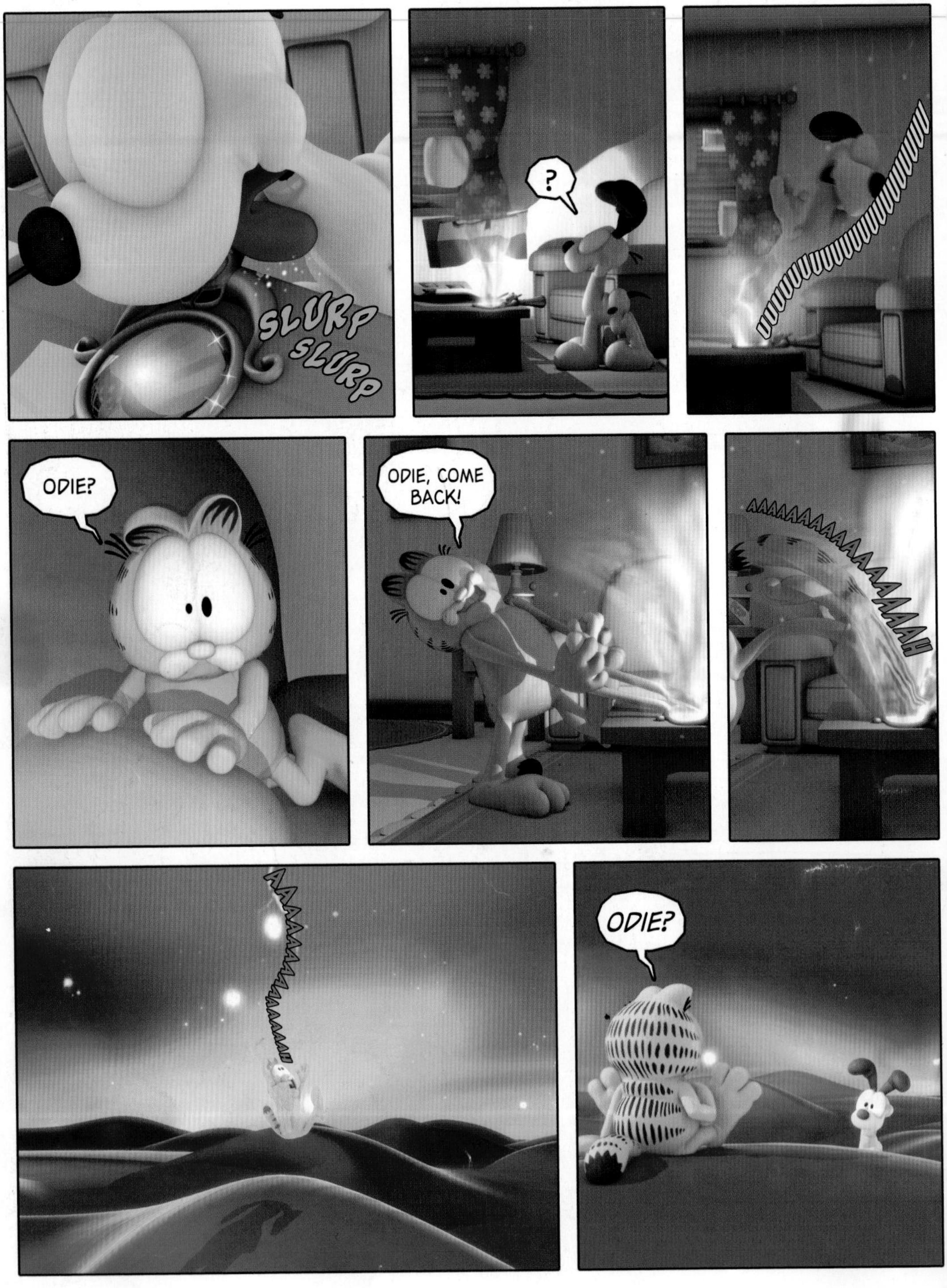
SLURP
SLURP
?
UUUUUUUUUUUUUUUUUUUUUUUUUUUUUU
ODIE?
ODIE, COME BACK!
AAAAAAAAAAAAAAAAAAAAAAH
AAAAAAAAAAAAAAAAAAA!!
ODIE?

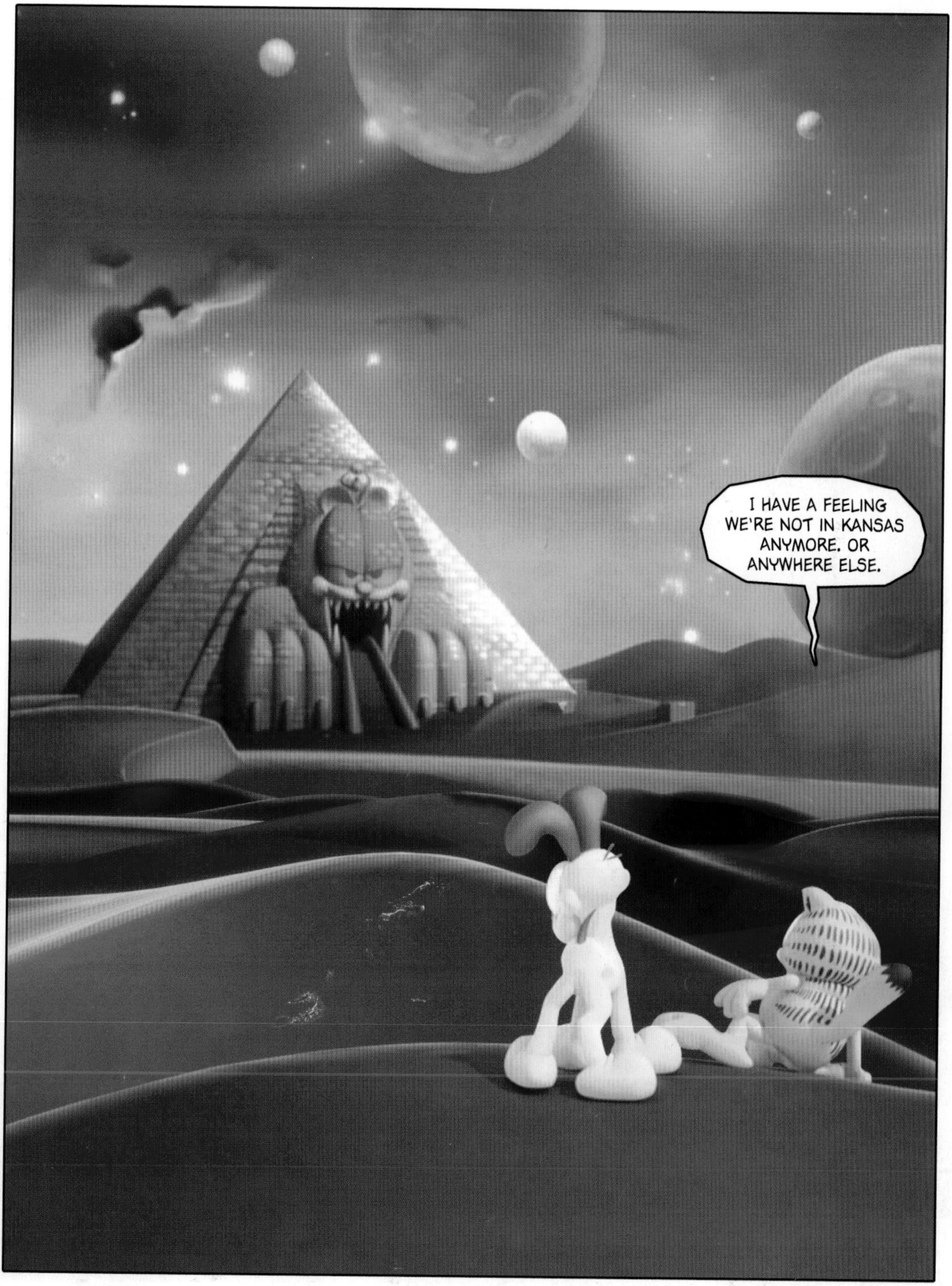
I HAVE A FEELING WE'RE NOT IN KANSAS ANYMORE. OR ANYWHERE ELSE.

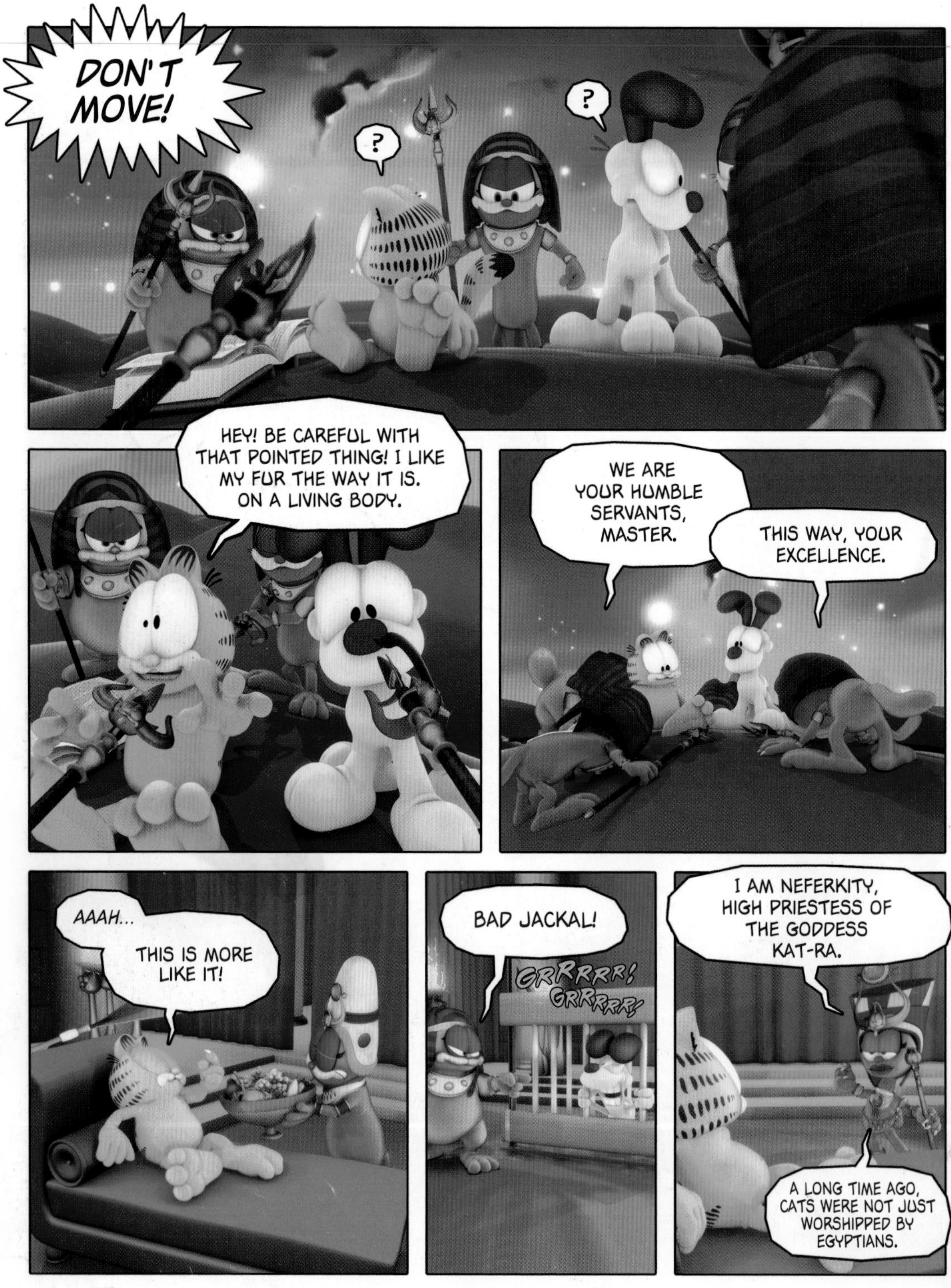
DON'T MOVE!
?
?
HEY! BE CAREFUL WITH THAT POINTED THING! I LIKE MY FUR THE WAY IT IS. ON A LIVING BODY.
WE ARE YOUR HUMBLE SERVANTS, MASTER.
THIS WAY, YOUR EXCELLENCE.
AAAH...
THIS IS MORE LIKE IT!
BAD JACKAL!
GRRRRR! GRRRRR!
I AM NEFERKITY, HIGH PRIESTESS OF THE GODDESS KAT-RA.
A LONG TIME AGO, CATS WERE NOT JUST WORSHIPPED BY EGYPTIANS.

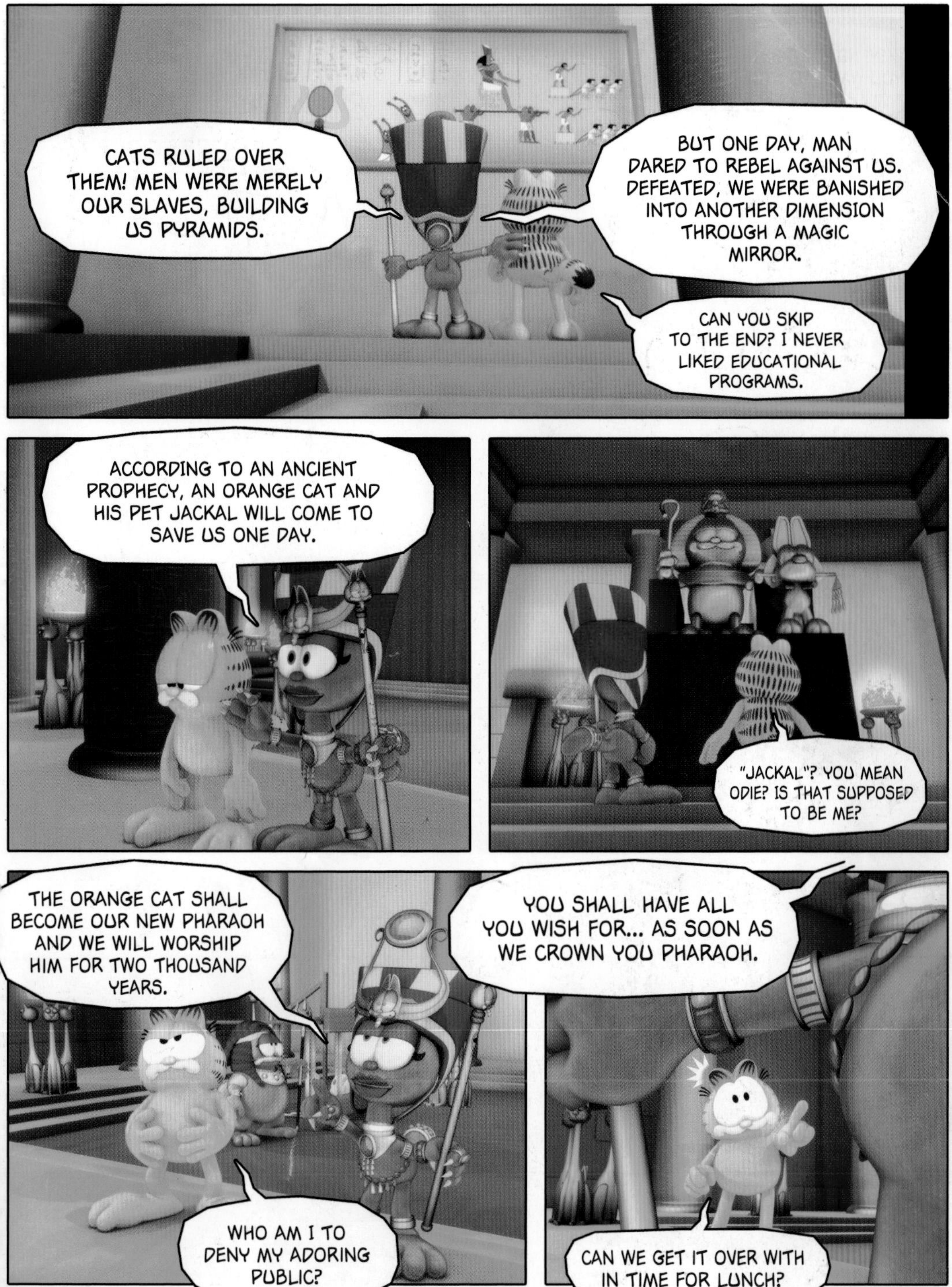
CATS RULED OVER THEM! MEN WERE MERELY OUR SLAVES, BUILDING US PYRAMIDS.
BUT ONE DAY, MAN DARED TO REBEL AGAINST US. DEFEATED, WE WERE BANISHED INTO ANOTHER DIMENSION THROUGH A MAGIC MIRROR.
CAN YOU SKIP TO THE END? I NEVER LIKED EDUCATIONAL PROGRAMS.
ACCORDING TO AN ANCIENT PROPHECY, AN ORANGE CAT AND HIS PET JACKAL WILL COME TO SAVE US ONE DAY.
"JACKAL"? YOU MEAN ODIE? IS THAT SUPPOSED TO BE ME?
THE ORANGE CAT SHALL BECOME OUR NEW PHARAOH AND WE WILL WORSHIP HIM FOR TWO THOUSAND YEARS.
WHO AM I TO DENY MY ADORING PUBLIC?
YOU SHALL HAVE ALL YOU WISH FOR... AS SOON AS WE CROWN YOU PHARAOH.
CAN WE GET IT OVER WITH IN TIME FOR LUNCH?

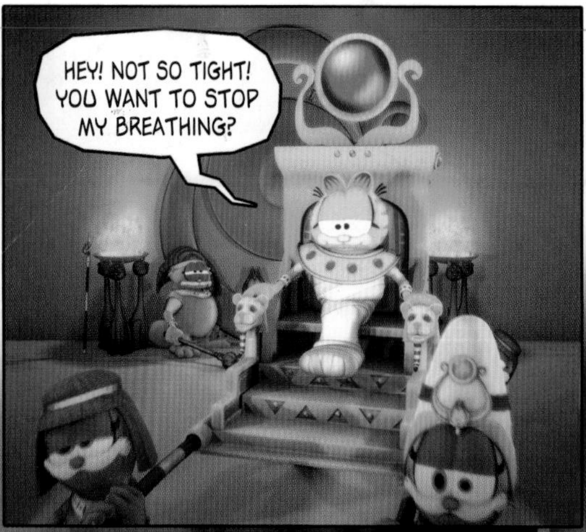
HEY! NOT SO TIGHT! YOU WANT TO STOP MY BREATHING?

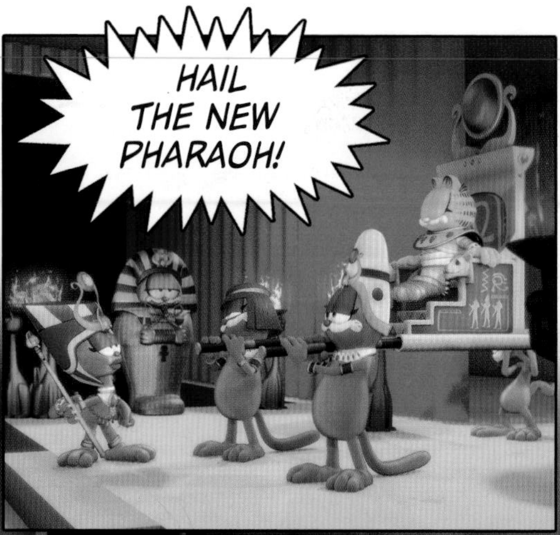
HAIL THE NEW PHARAOH!

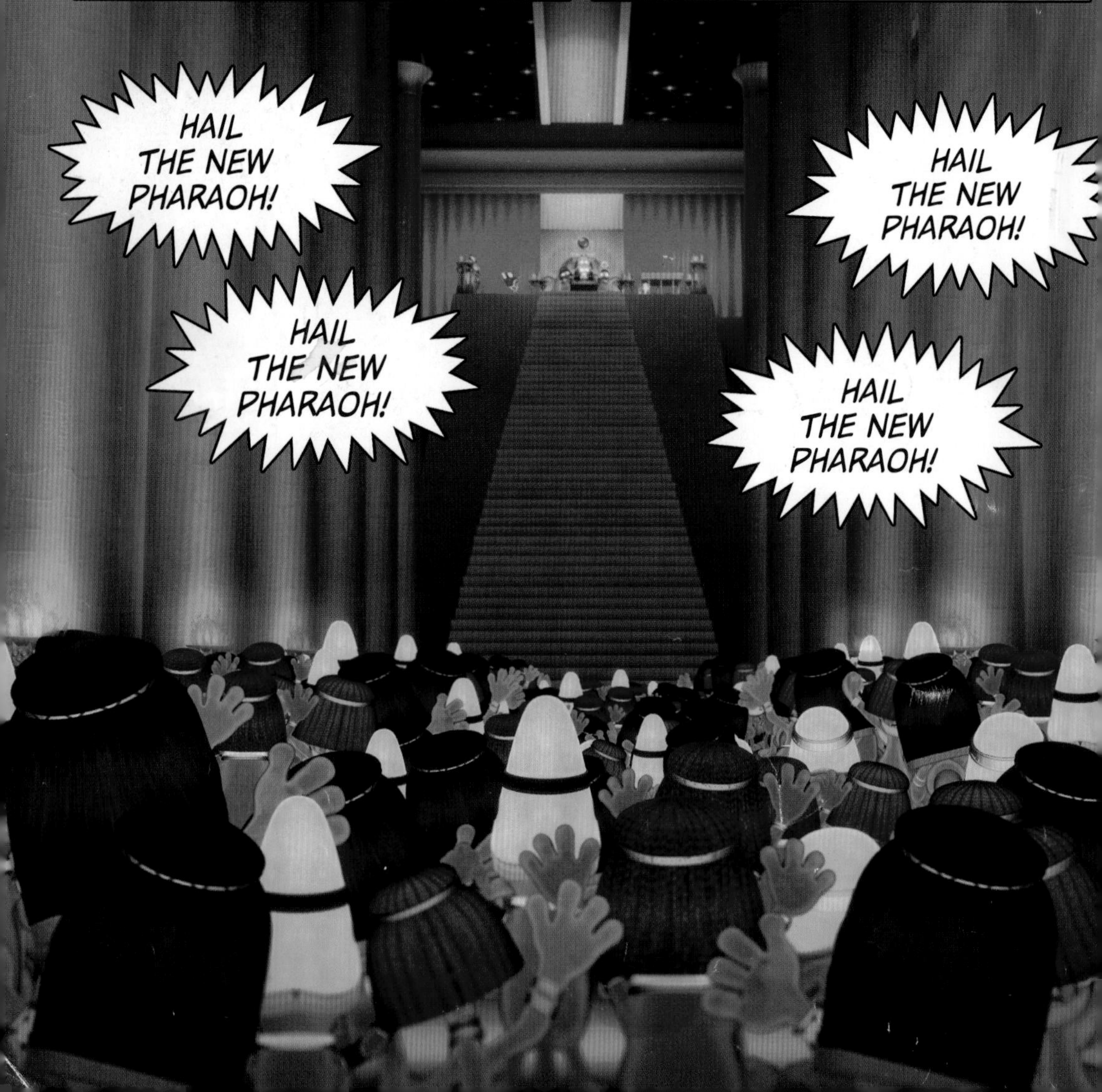
HAIL THE NEW PHARAOH!
HAIL THE NEW PHARAOH!
HAIL THE NEW PHARAOH!
HAIL THE NEW PHARAOH!

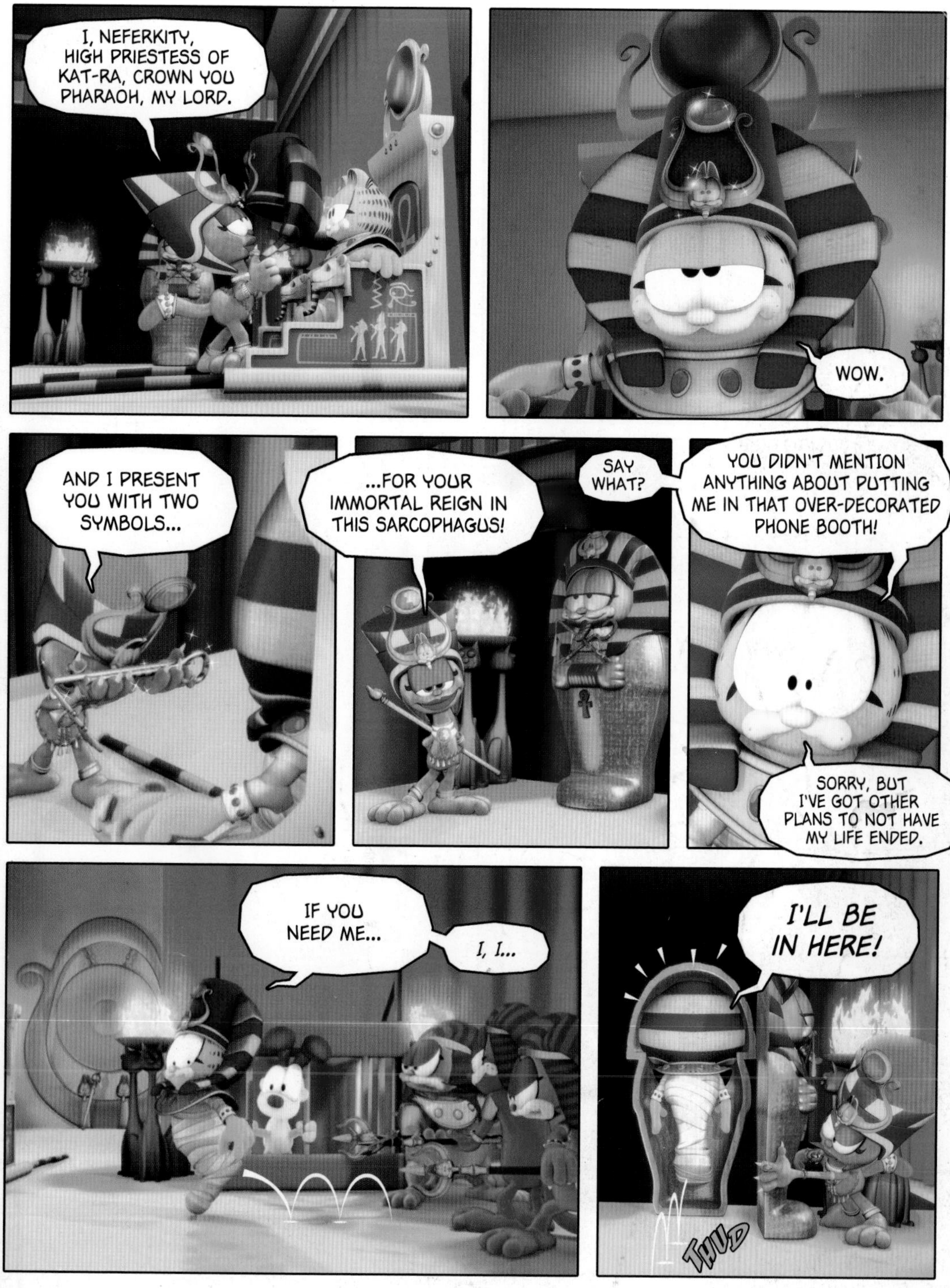
I, NEFERKITY, HIGH PRIESTESS OF KAT-RA, CROWN YOU PHARAOH, MY LORD.
WOW.
AND I PRESENT YOU WITH TWO SYMBOLS...
...FOR YOUR IMMORTAL REIGN IN THIS SARCOPHAGUS!
SAY WHAT?
YOU DIDN'T MENTION ANYTHING ABOUT PUTTING ME IN THAT OVER-DECORATED PHONE BOOTH!
SORRY, BUT I'VE GOT OTHER PLANS TO NOT HAVE MY LIFE ENDED.
IF YOU NEED ME...
I, I...
I'LL BE IN HERE!
THUD

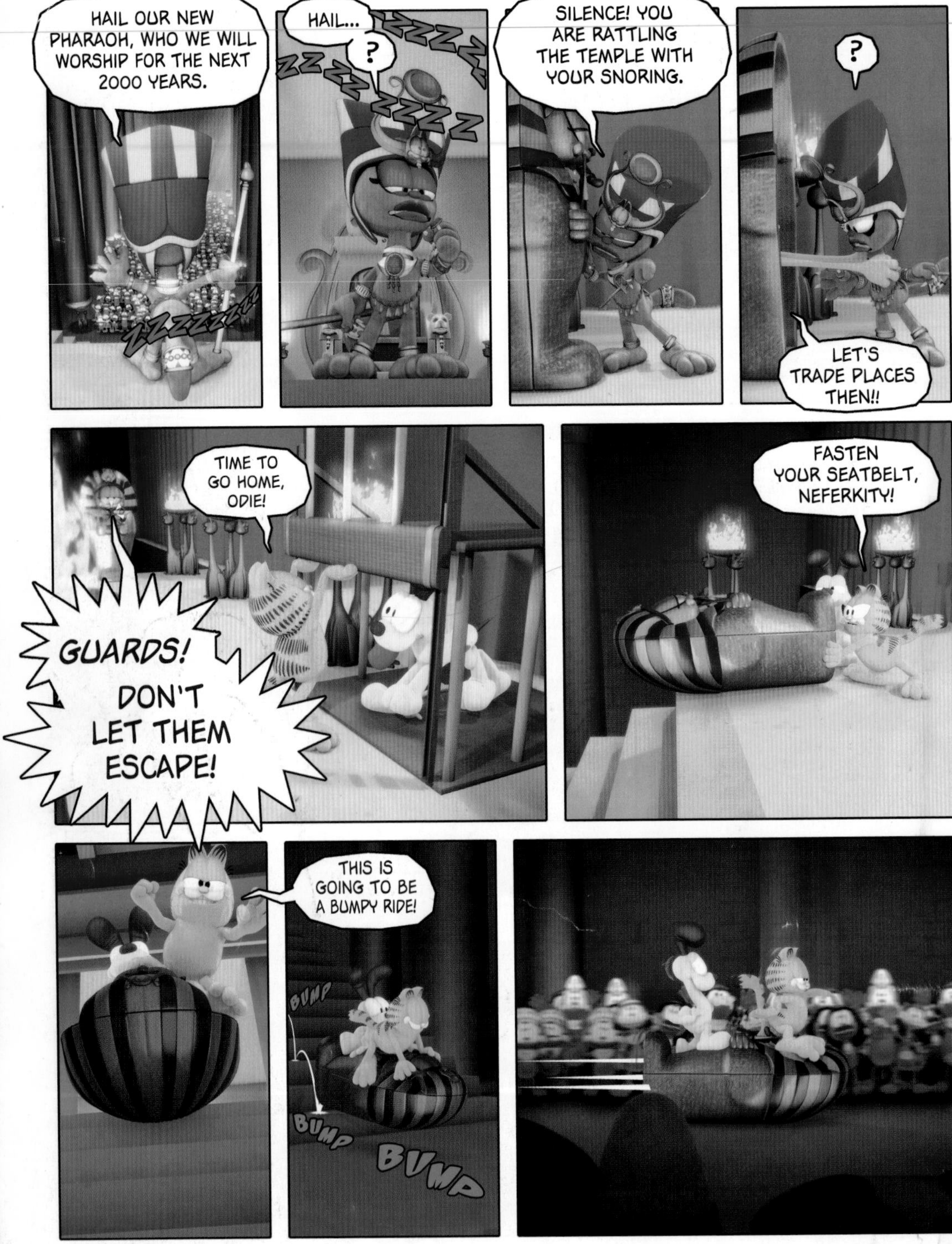
HAIL OUR NEW PHARAOH, WHO WE WILL WORSHIP FOR THE NEXT 2000 YEARS.
ZZZZZZZZ
HAIL...
ZZZZZ
ZZZZ
?
ZZZZZ
SILENCE! YOU ARE RATTLING THE TEMPLE WITH YOUR SNORING.
?
LET'S TRADE PLACES THEN!!
TIME TO GO HOME, ODIE!
GUARDS! DON'T LET THEM ESCAPE!
FASTEN YOUR SEATBELT, NEFERKITY!
THIS IS GOING TO BE A BUMPY RIDE!
BUMP
BUMP
BUMP

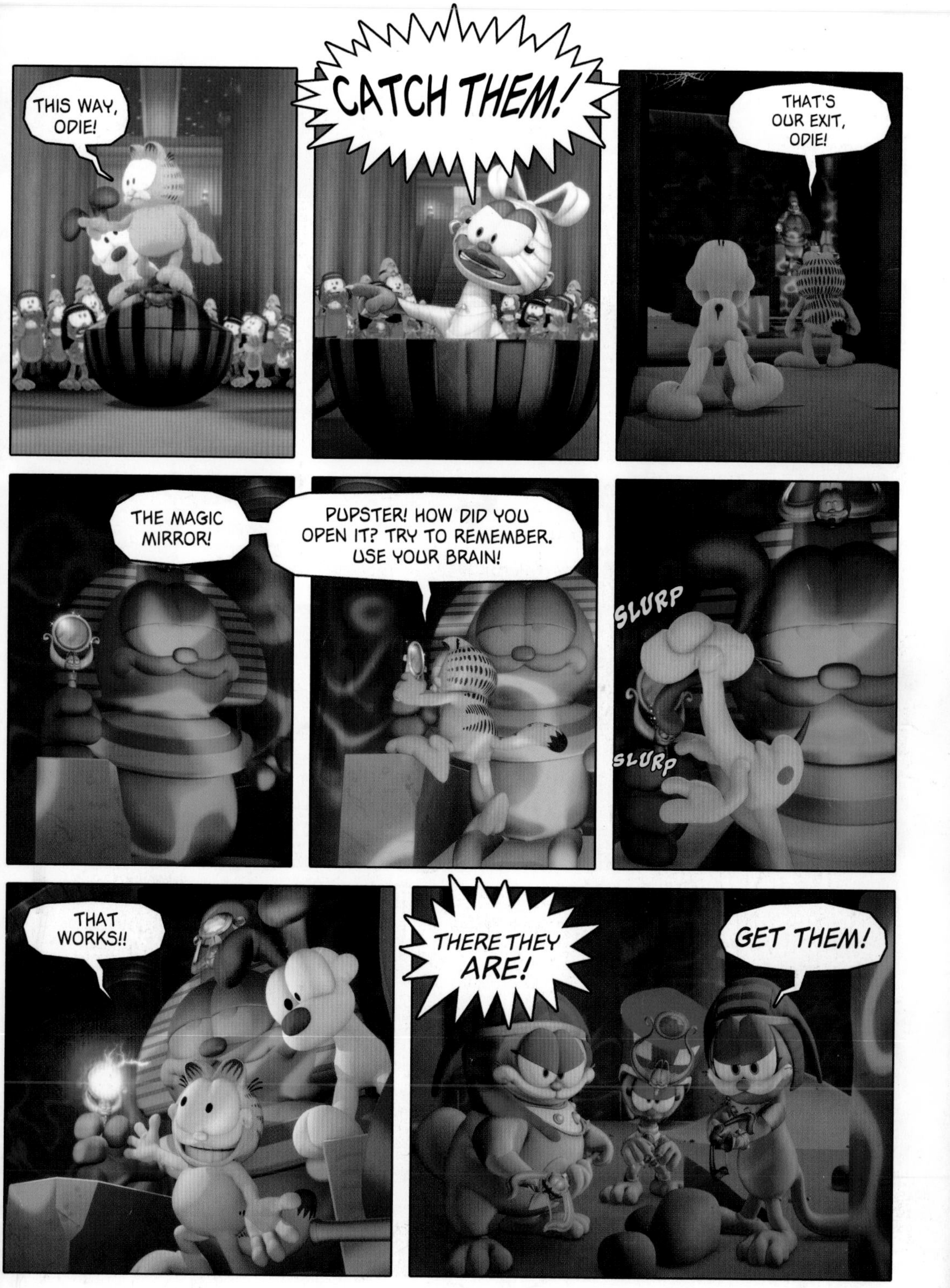
THIS WAY, ODIE!
CATCH THEM!
THAT'S OUR EXIT, ODIE!
THE MAGIC MIRROR!
PUPSTER! HOW DID YOU OPEN IT? TRY TO REMEMBER. USE YOUR BRAIN!
SLURP
SLURP
THAT WORKS!!
THERE THEY ARE!
GET THEM!

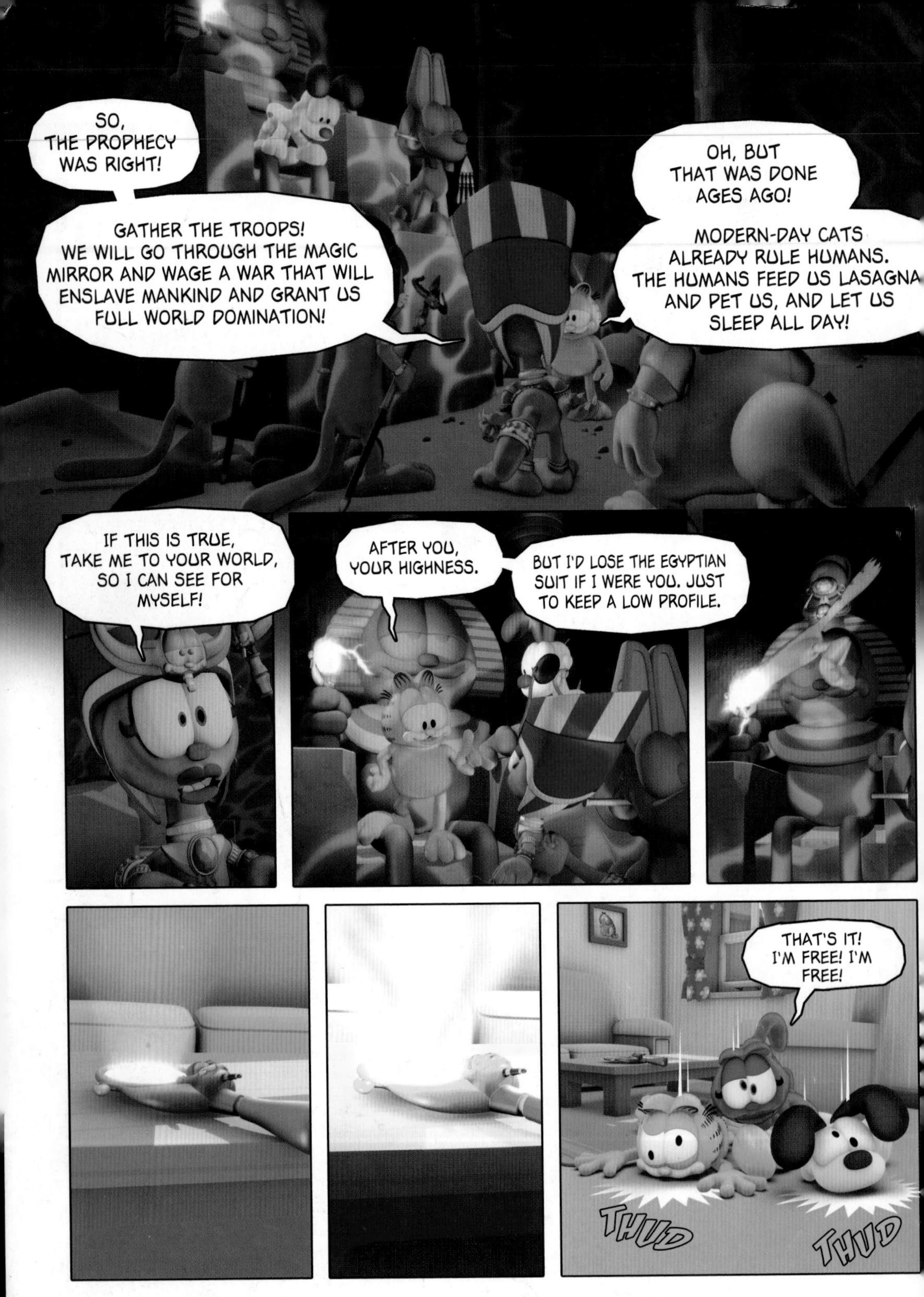
SO, THE PROPHECY WAS RIGHT!
GATHER THE TROOPS! WE WILL GO THROUGH THE MAGIC MIRROR AND WAGE A WAR THAT WILL ENSLAVE MANKIND AND GRANT US FULL WORLD DOMINATION!
OH, BUT THAT WAS DONE AGES AGO!
MODERN-DAY CATS ALREADY RULE HUMANS. THE HUMANS FEED US LASAGNA AND PET US, AND LET US SLEEP ALL DAY!
IF THIS IS TRUE, TAKE ME TO YOUR WORLD, SO I CAN SEE FOR MYSELF!
AFTER YOU, YOUR HIGHNESS.
BUT I'D LOSE THE EGYPTIAN SUIT IF I WERE YOU. JUST TO KEEP A LOW PROFILE.
THAT'S IT! I'M FREE! I'M FREE!
THUD
THUD

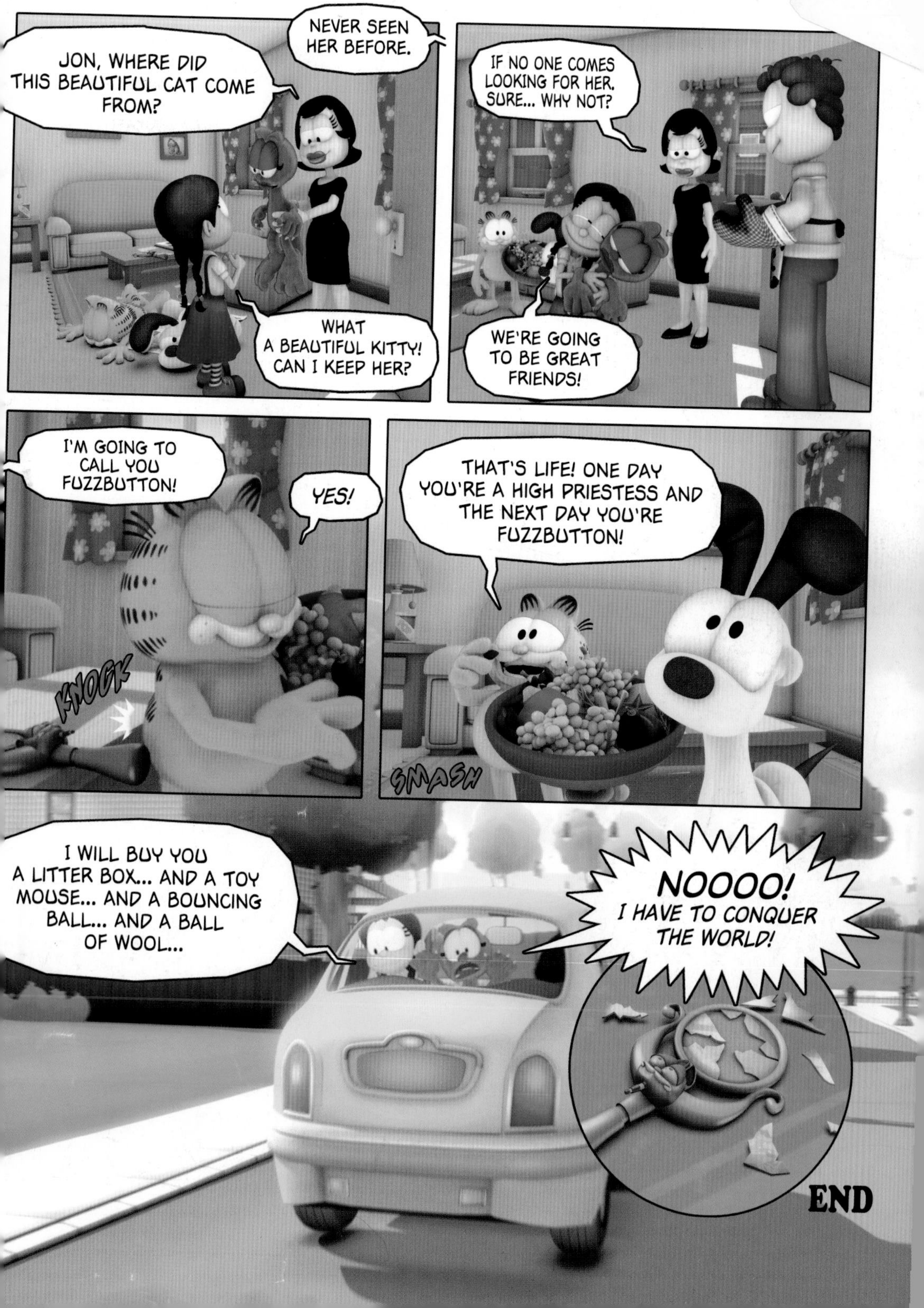
JON, WHERE DID THIS BEAUTIFUL CAT COME FROM?
NEVER SEEN HER BEFORE.
WHAT A BEAUTIFUL KITTY! CAN I KEEP HER?
IF NO ONE COMES LOOKING FOR HER. SURE... WHY NOT?
WE'RE GOING TO BE GREAT FRIENDS!
I'M GOING TO CALL YOU FUZZBUTTON!
YES!
KNOCK
THAT'S LIFE! ONE DAY YOU'RE A HIGH PRIESTESS AND THE NEXT DAY YOU'RE FUZZBUTTON!
SMASH
I WILL BUY YOU A LITTER BOX... AND A TOY MOUSE... AND A BOUNCING BALL... AND A BALL OF WOOL...
NOOOO! I HAVE TO CONQUER THE WORLD!
END

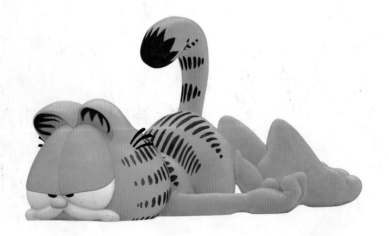

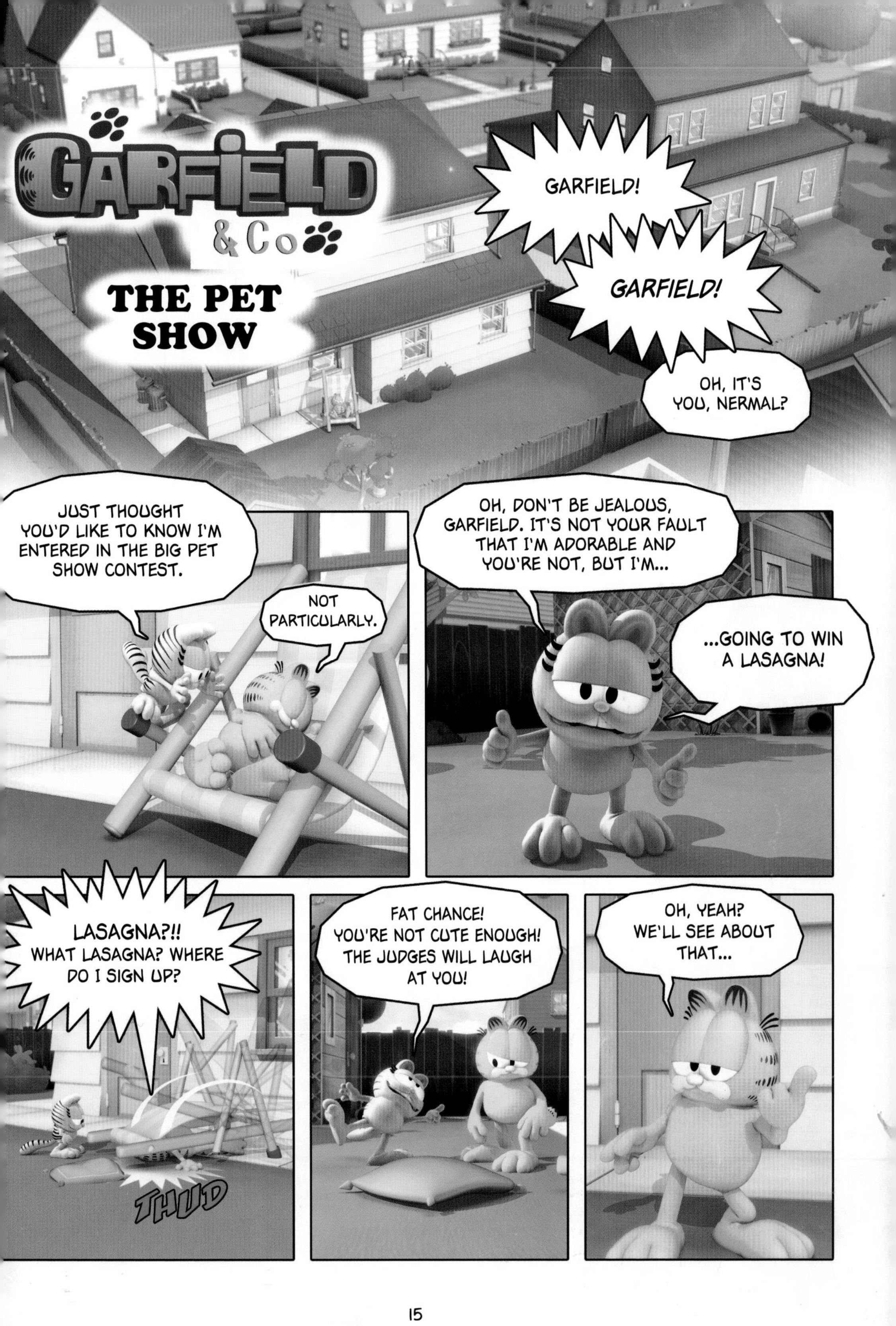
GARFIELD & Co
THE PET SHOW
GARFIELD!
GARFIELD!
OH, IT'S YOU, NERMAL?
JUST THOUGHT YOU'D LIKE TO KNOW I'M ENTERED IN THE BIG PET SHOW CONTEST.
NOT PARTICULARLY.
OH, DON'T BE JEALOUS, GARFIELD. IT'S NOT YOUR FAULT THAT I'M ADORABLE AND YOU'RE NOT, BUT I'M...
...GOING TO WIN A LASAGNA!
LASAGNA?!! WHAT LASAGNA? WHERE DO I SIGN UP?
THUD
FAT CHANCE! YOU'RE NOT CUTE ENOUGH! THE JUDGES WILL LAUGH AT YOU!
OH, YEAH? WE'LL SEE ABOUT THAT...

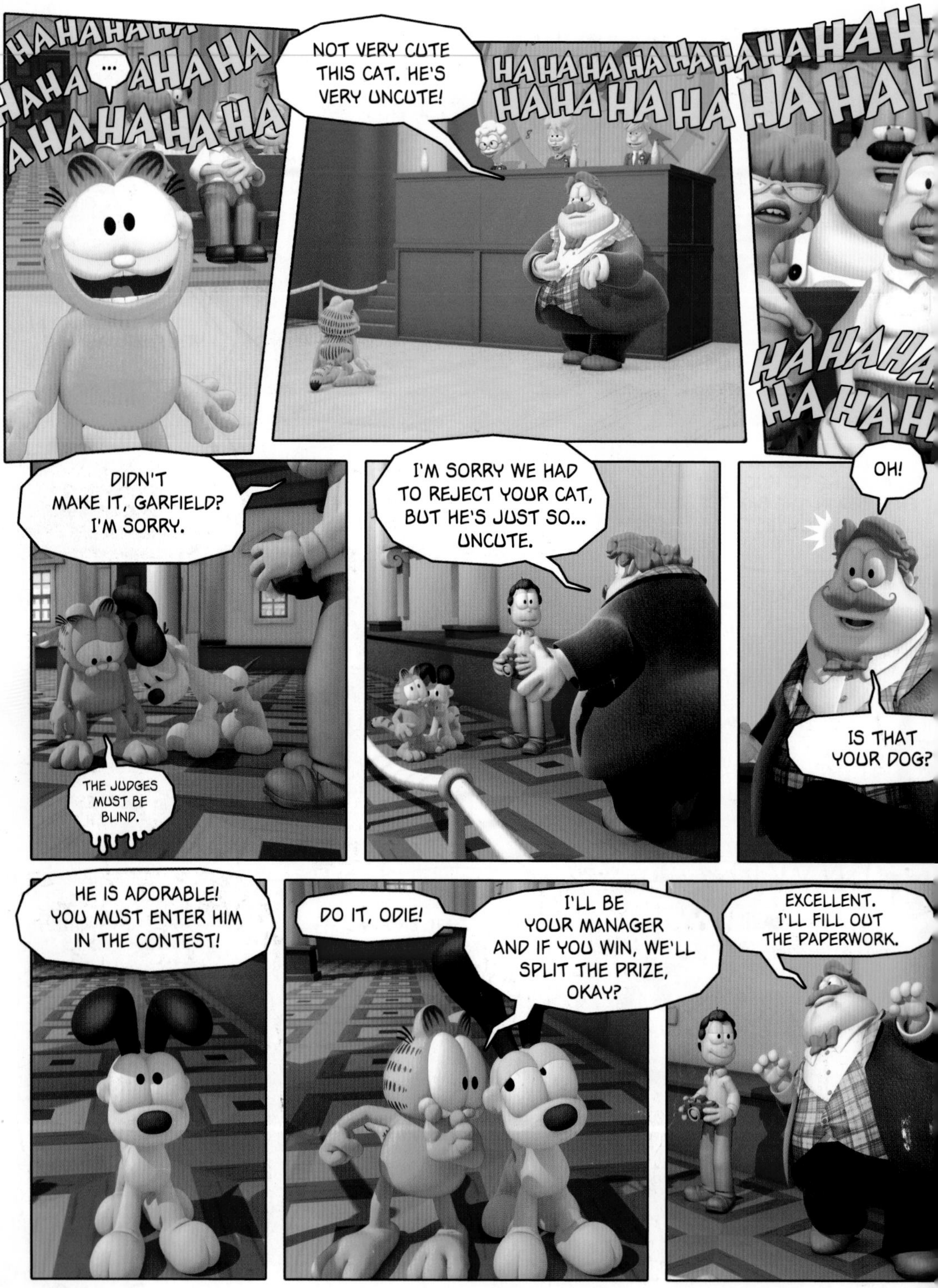
HAHAHAHAHA
HAHA ... AHAHA
AHAHAHAHA
NOT VERY CUTE THIS CAT. HE'S VERY UNCUTE!
HAHAHAHAHAHAHAHAHAHAH
HAHAHAHAHAHAH
HAHAHA
HAHAH
DIDN'T MAKE IT, GARFIELD? I'M SORRY.
THE JUDGES MUST BE BLIND.
I'M SORRY WE HAD TO REJECT YOUR CAT, BUT HE'S JUST SO... UNCUTE.
OH!
IS THAT YOUR DOG?
HE IS ADORABLE! YOU MUST ENTER HIM IN THE CONTEST!
DO IT, ODIE!
I'LL BE YOUR MANAGER AND IF YOU WIN, WE'LL SPLIT THE PRIZE, OKAY?
EXCELLENT. I'LL FILL OUT THE PAPERWORK.

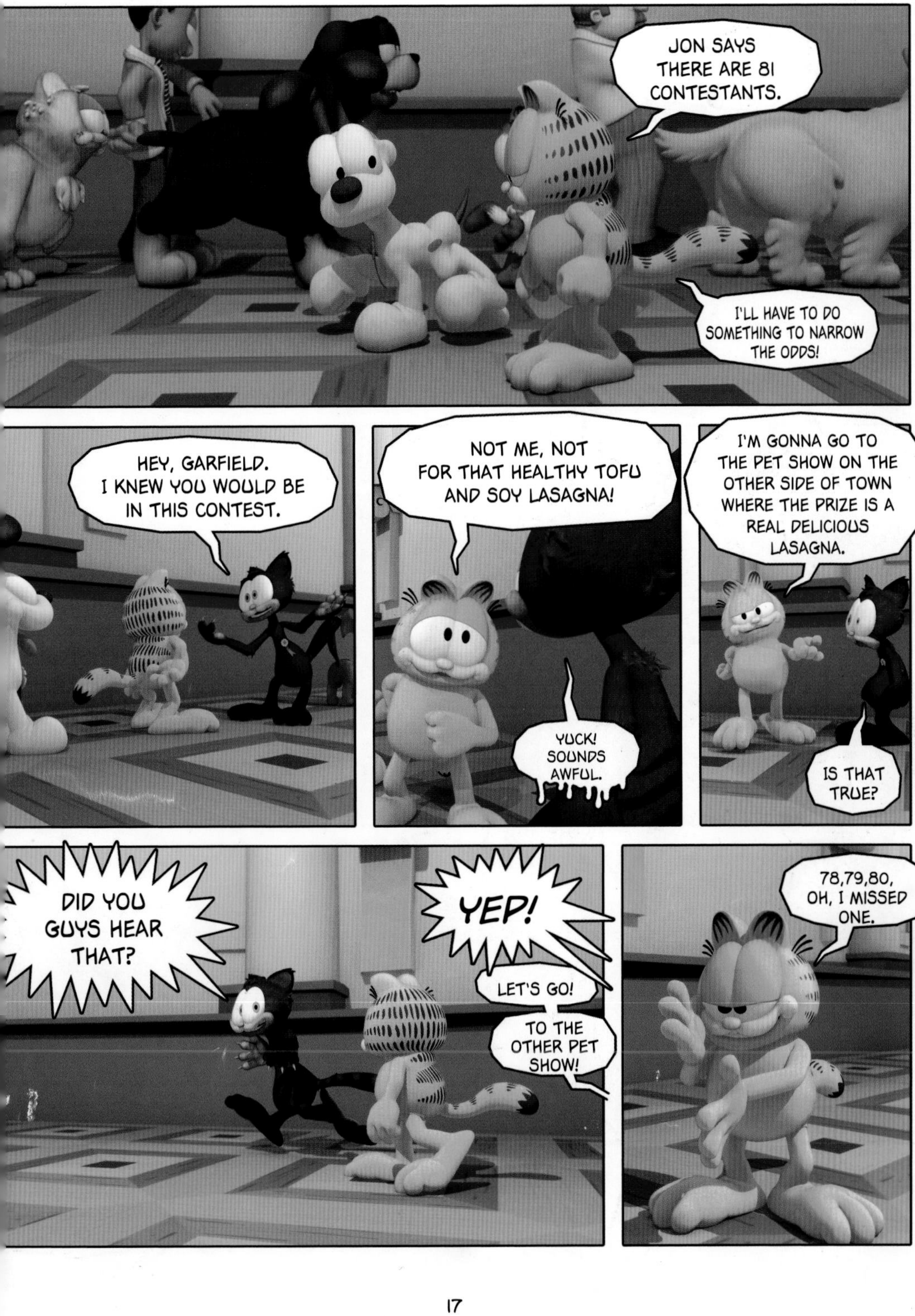
JON SAYS THERE ARE 81 CONTESTANTS.
I'LL HAVE TO DO SOMETHING TO NARROW THE ODDS!
HEY, GARFIELD. I KNEW YOU WOULD BE IN THIS CONTEST.
NOT ME, NOT FOR THAT HEALTHY TOFU AND SOY LASAGNA!
YUCK! SOUNDS AWFUL.
I'M GONNA GO TO THE PET SHOW ON THE OTHER SIDE OF TOWN WHERE THE PRIZE IS A REAL DELICIOUS LASAGNA.
IS THAT TRUE?
DID YOU GUYS HEAR THAT?
YEP!
LET'S GO!
TO THE OTHER PET SHOW!
78,79,80, OH, I MISSED ONE.

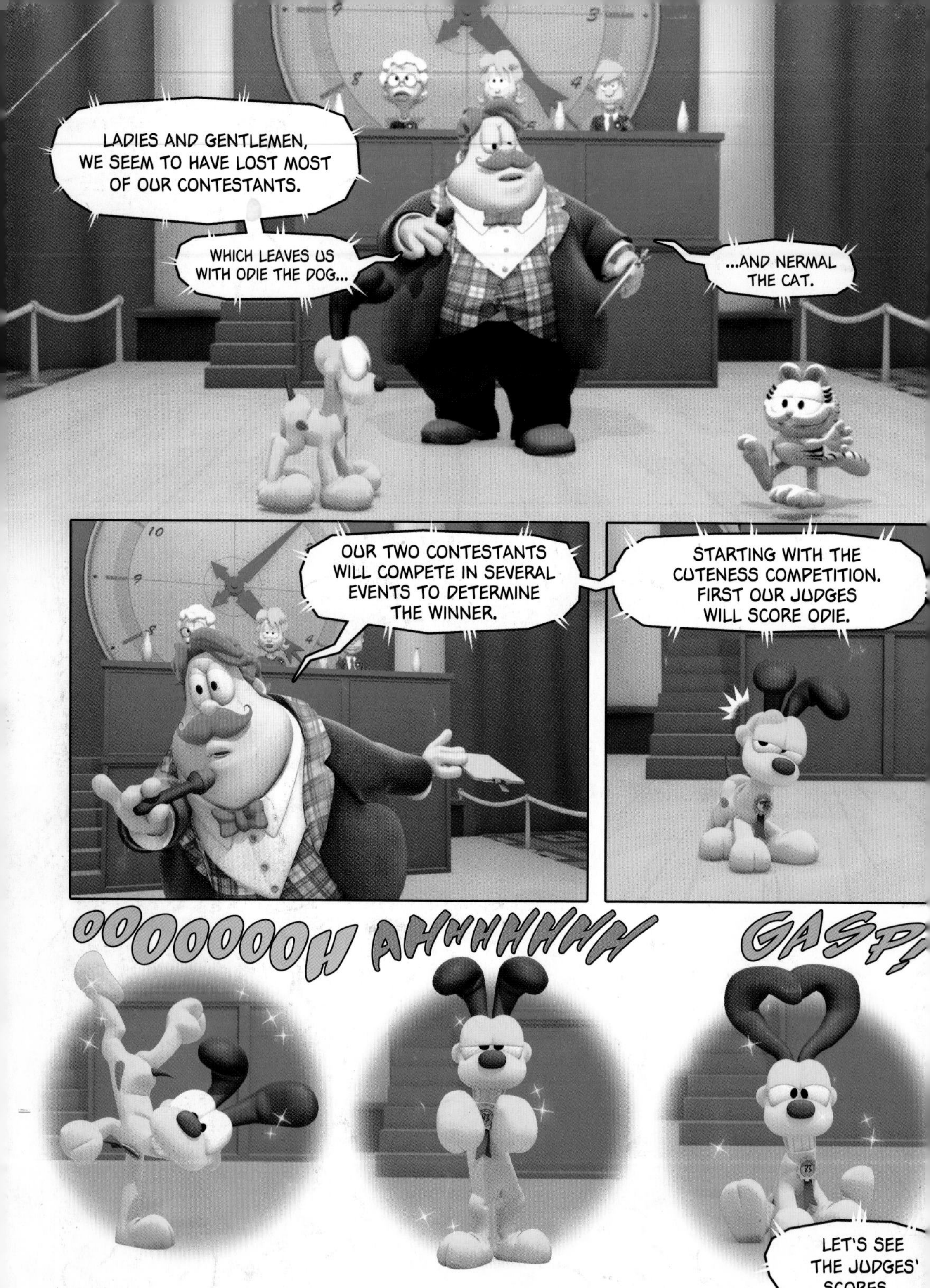
LADIES AND GENTLEMEN, WE SEEM TO HAVE LOST MOST OF OUR CONTESTANTS.
WHICH LEAVES US WITH ODIE THE DOG...
...AND NERMAL THE CAT.
OUR TWO CONTESTANTS WILL COMPETE IN SEVERAL EVENTS TO DETERMINE THE WINNER.
STARTING WITH THE CUTENESS COMPETITION. FIRST OUR JUDGES WILL SCORE ODIE.
OOOOOOOOH
AHHHHHHH
GASP!
LET'S SEE THE JUDGES' SCORES...

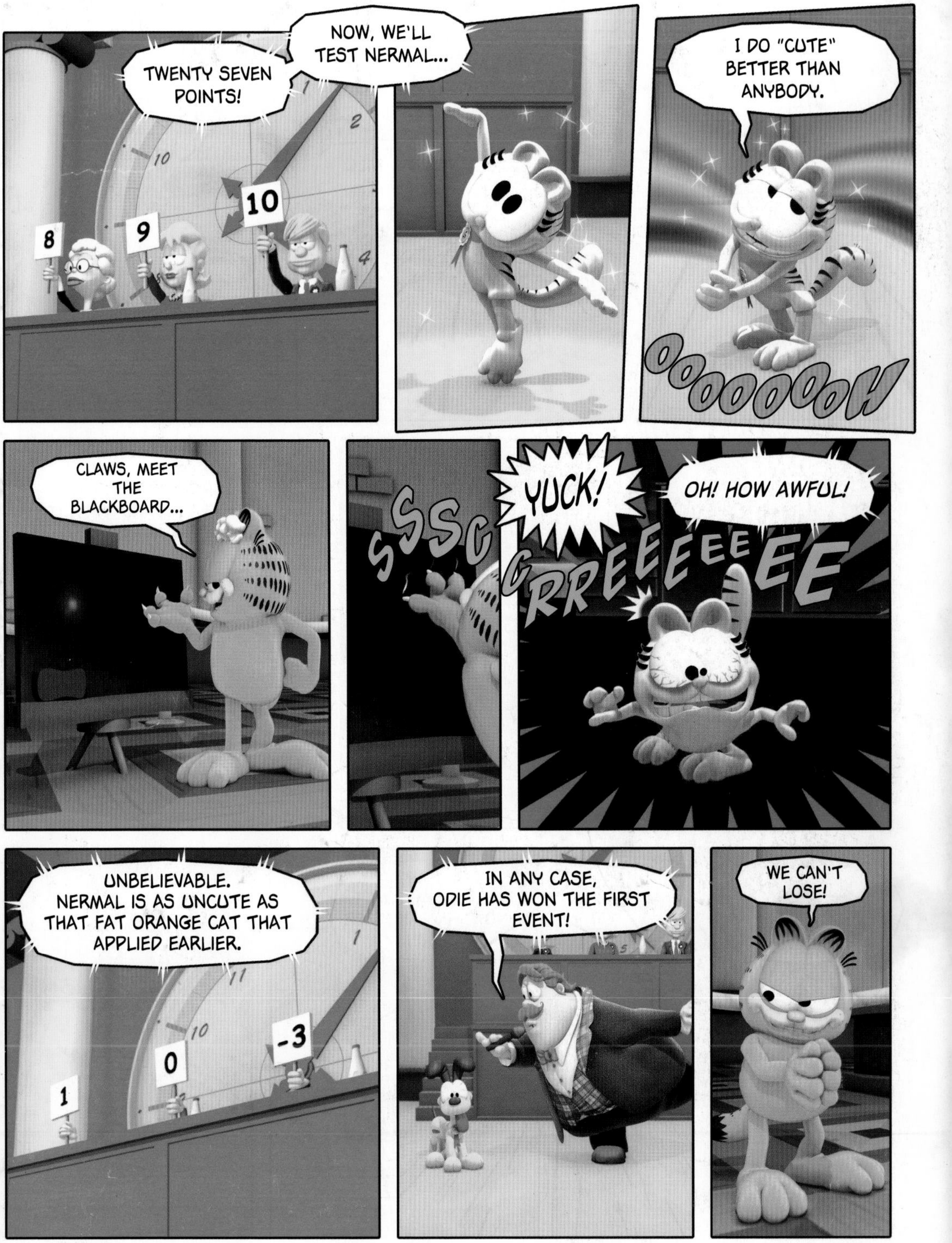

TWENTY SEVEN POINTS!
NOW, WE'LL TEST NERMAL...
8
9
10
I DO "CUTE" BETTER THAN ANYBODY.
OOOOOOOH
CLAWS, MEET THE BLACKBOARD...
SSSC
YUCK!
CRREEEEEEEE
OH! HOW AWFUL!
UNBELIEVABLE. NERMAL IS AS UNCUTE AS THAT FAT ORANGE CAT THAT APPLIED EARLIER.
1
0
-3
IN ANY CASE, ODIE HAS WON THE FIRST EVENT!
WE CAN'T LOSE!

THE NEXT EVENT WILL BE BASED ON INTELLIGENCE.

YOU HAVE TO FIND TWO MATCHING OBJECTS IN THIS PILE.

NERMAL WILL GO FIRST.

ON YOUR MARK, GET SET...

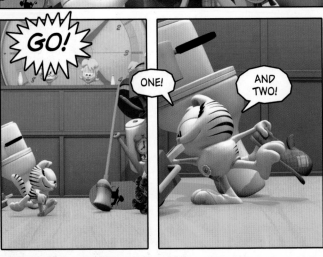

GO!

ONE!

AND TWO!

AND NERMAL FINDS ONE SLIPPER AND THEN ITS MATCH IN 7 SECONDS!

ALL RIGHT, BOY. GET AN ITEM FROM THE PILE!

YOUR TURN, ODIE!

OKAY, A BASEBALL MITT. NOW, FIND ANOTHER ONE!

NOOOO!

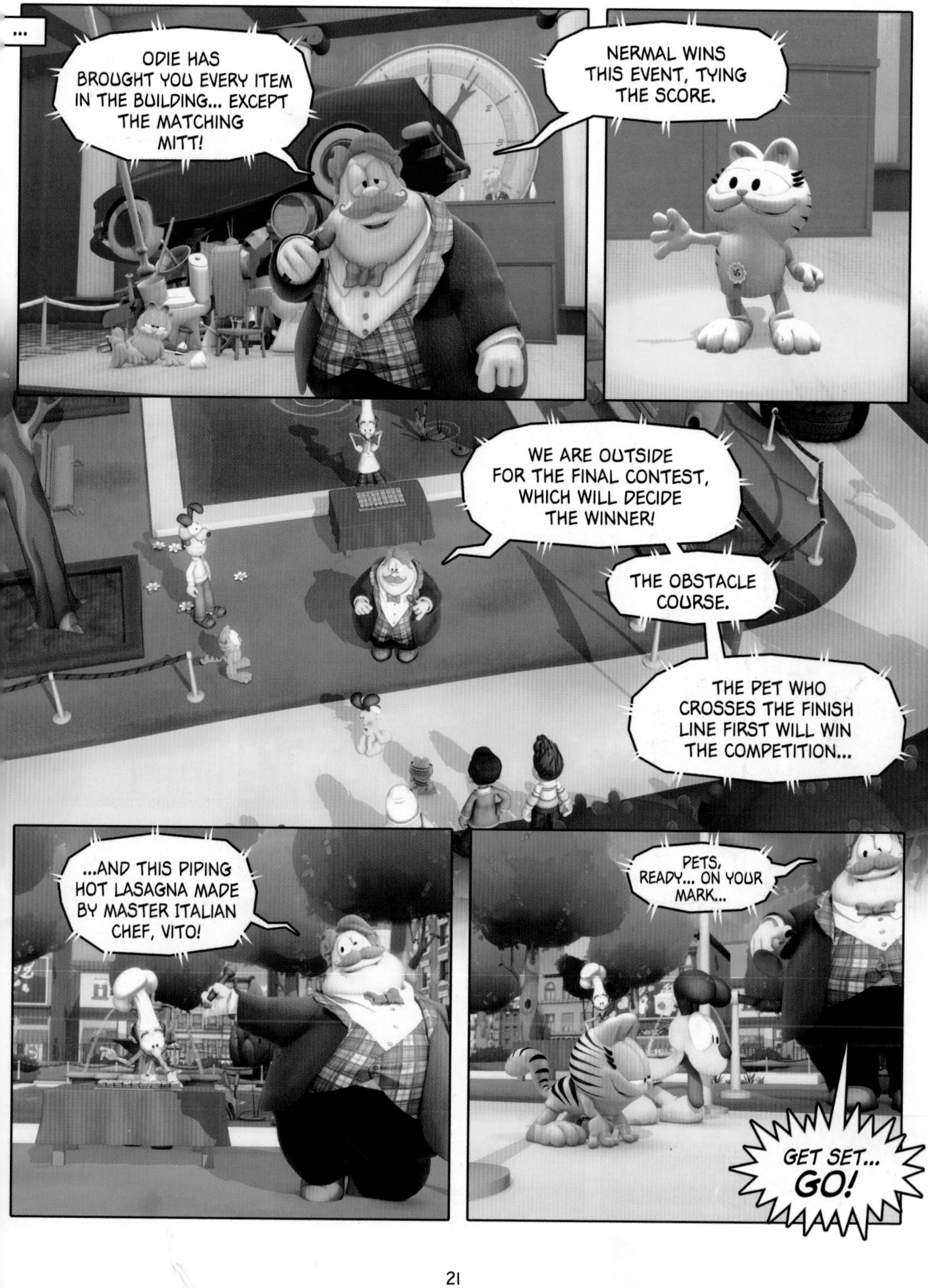
...
ODIE HAS BROUGHT YOU EVERY ITEM IN THE BUILDING... EXCEPT THE MATCHING MITT!
NERMAL WINS THIS EVENT, TYING THE SCORE.
WE ARE OUTSIDE FOR THE FINAL CONTEST, WHICH WILL DECIDE THE WINNER!
THE OBSTACLE COURSE.
THE PET WHO CROSSES THE FINISH LINE FIRST WILL WIN THE COMPETITION...
...AND THIS PIPING HOT LASAGNA MADE BY MASTER ITALIAN CHEF, VITO!
PETS, READY... ON YOUR MARK...
GET SET... GO!

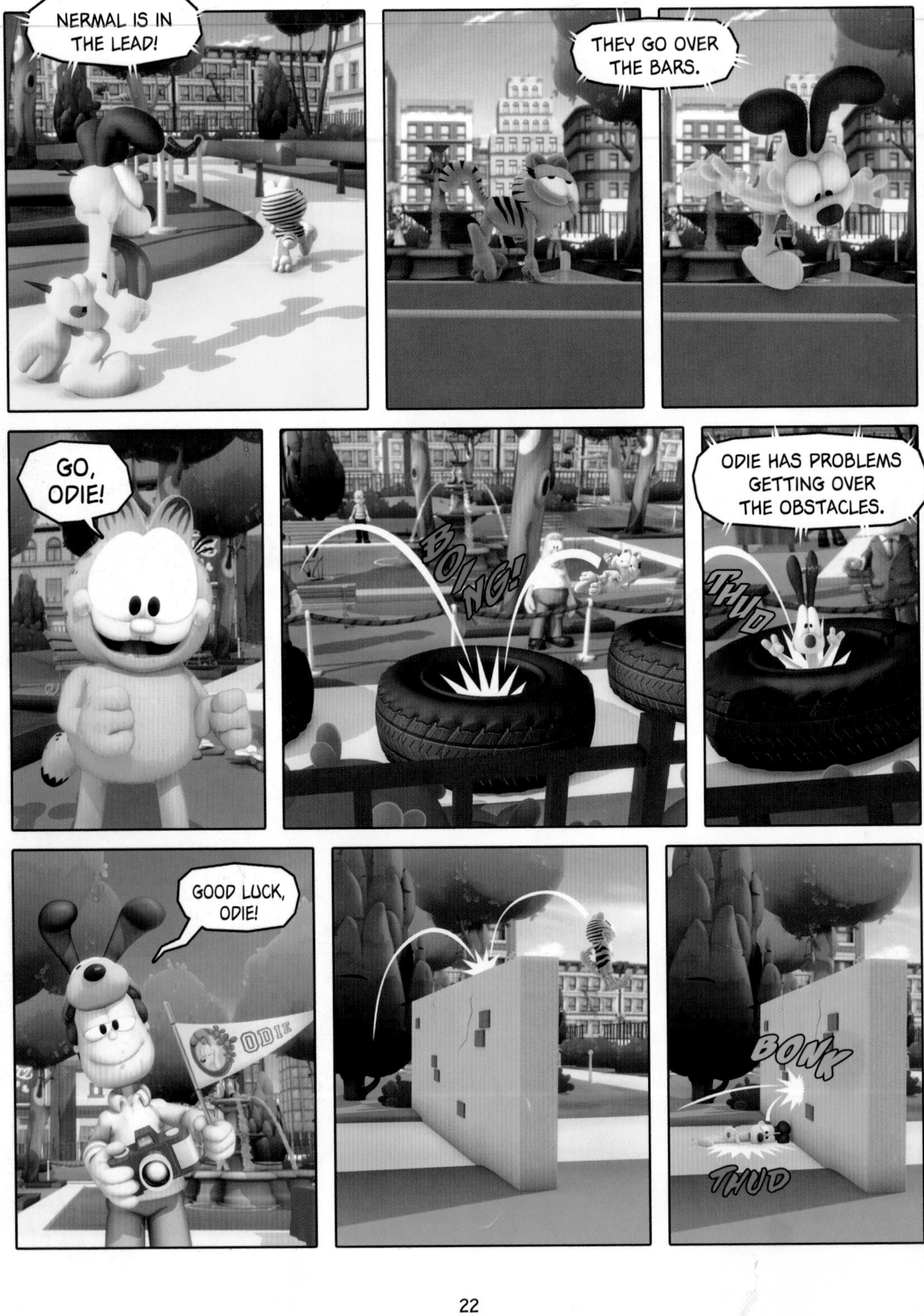
NERMAL IS IN THE LEAD!
THEY GO OVER THE BARS.
GO, ODIE!
BOING!
ODIE HAS PROBLEMS GETTING OVER THE OBSTACLES.
THUD
GOOD LUCK, ODIE!
ODIE
BONK
THUD

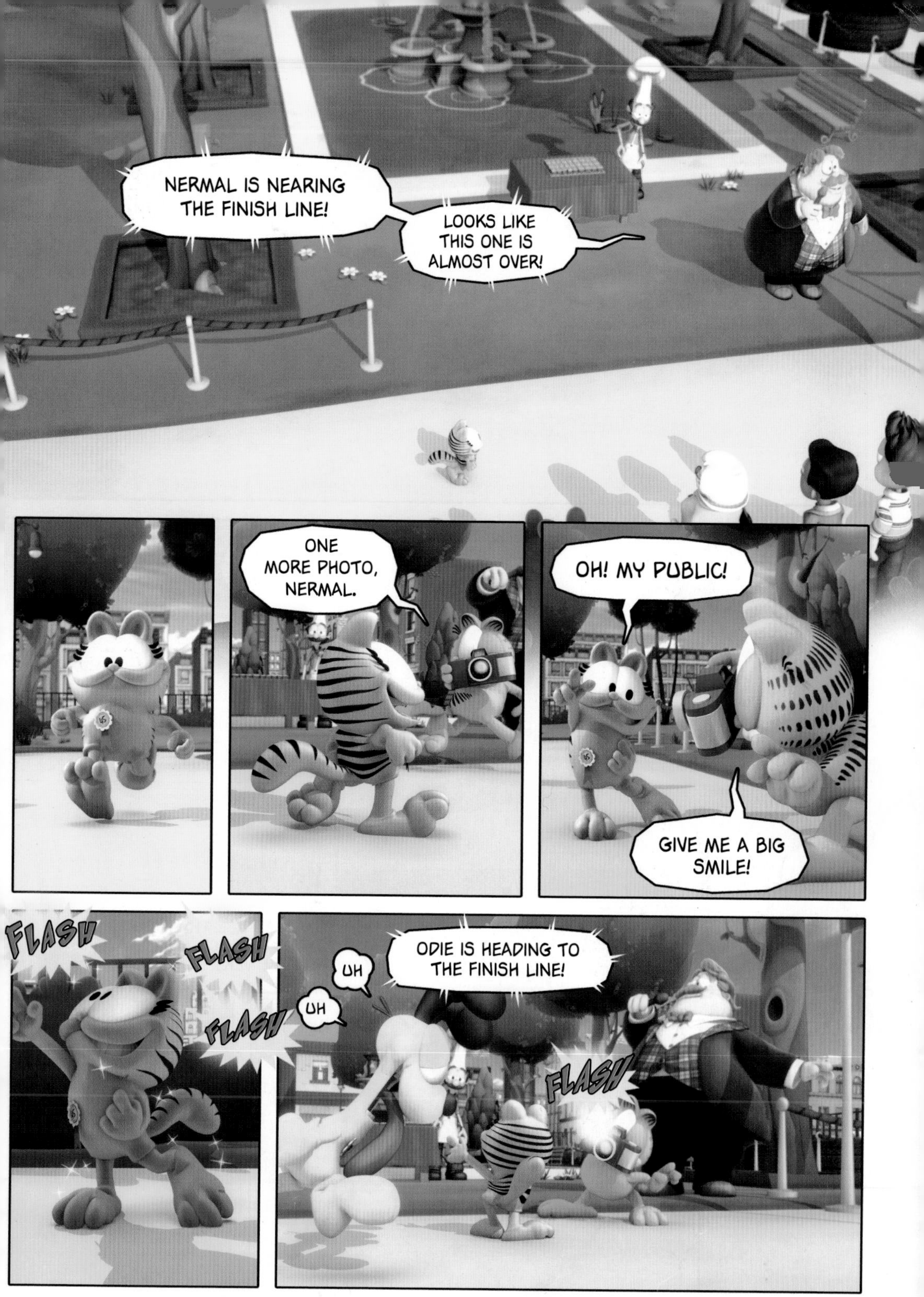
NERMAL IS NEARING THE FINISH LINE!
LOOKS LIKE THIS ONE IS ALMOST OVER!
ONE MORE PHOTO, NERMAL.
OH! MY PUBLIC!
GIVE ME A BIG SMILE!
FLASH
FLASH
FLASH
UH
UH
ODIE IS HEADING TO THE FINISH LINE!
FLASH

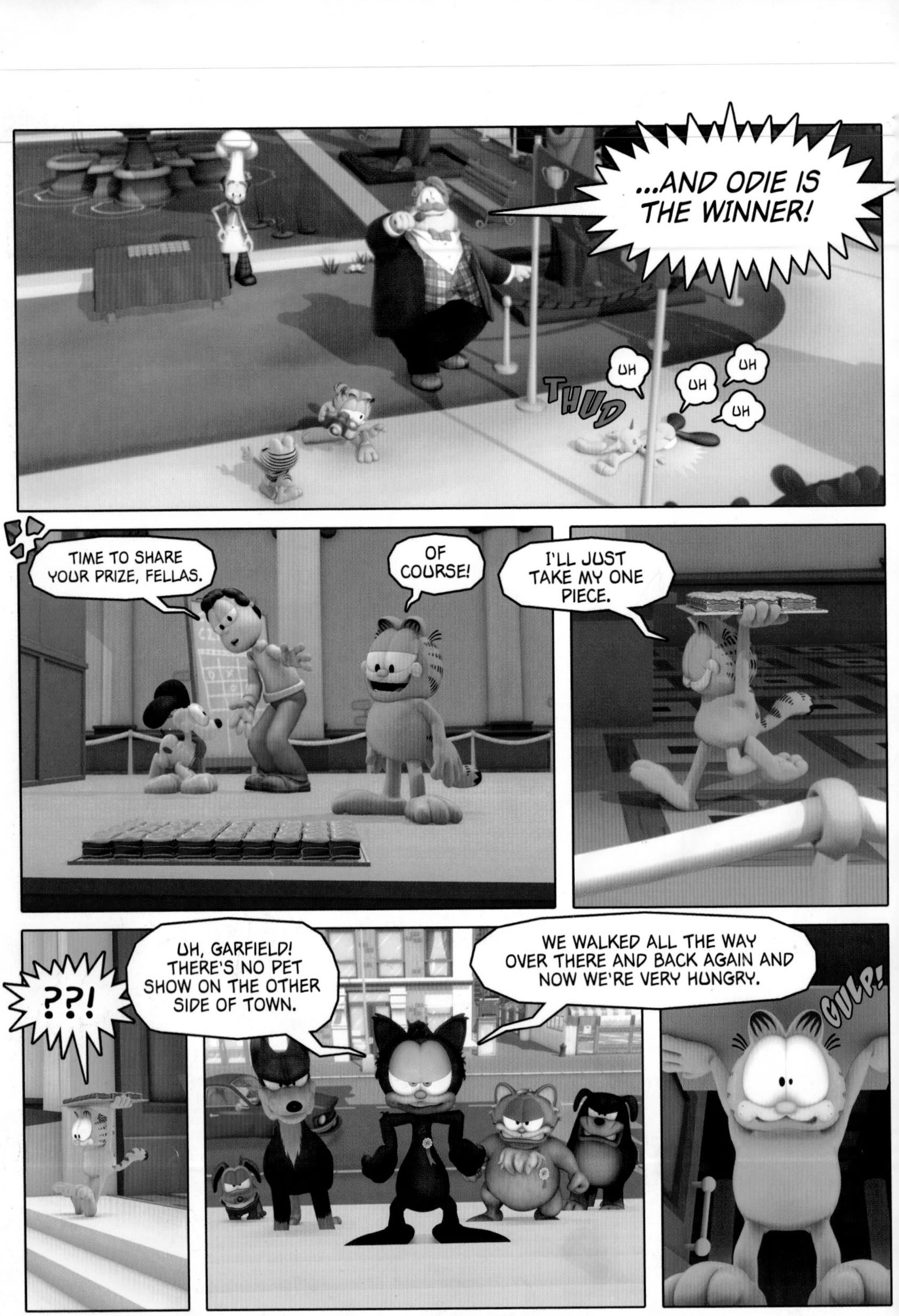
...AND ODIE IS THE WINNER!
UH
UH
UH
UH
THUD
TIME TO SHARE YOUR PRIZE, FELLAS.
OF COURSE!
I'LL JUST TAKE MY ONE PIECE.
??!
UH, GARFIELD! THERE'S NO PET SHOW ON THE OTHER SIDE OF TOWN.
WE WALKED ALL THE WAY OVER THERE AND BACK AGAIN AND NOW WE'RE VERY HUNGRY.
GULP!

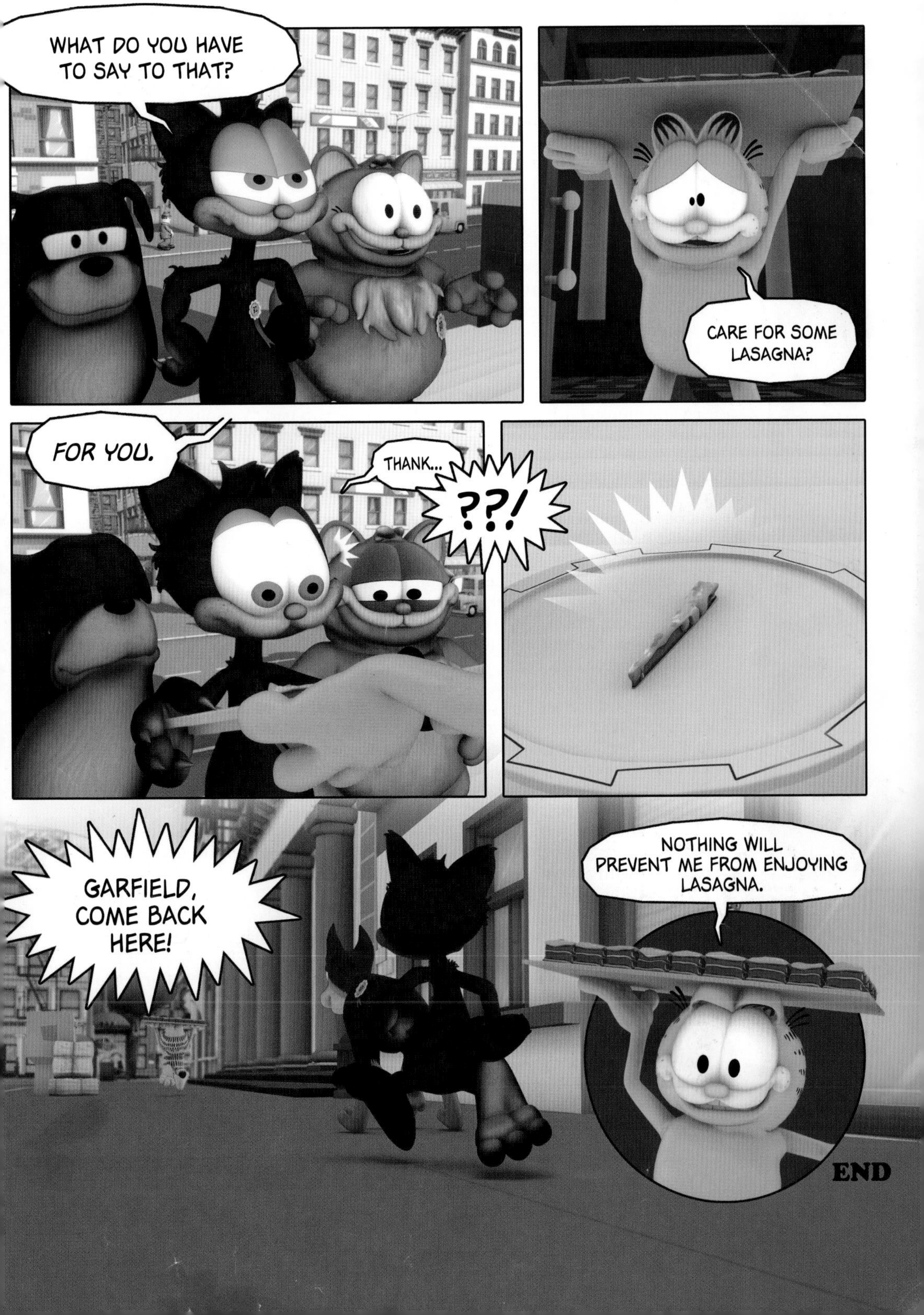

WHAT DO YOU HAVE TO SAY TO THAT?
CARE FOR SOME LASAGNA?
FOR YOU.
THANK...
??!
GARFIELD, COME BACK HERE!
NOTHING WILL PREVENT ME FROM ENJOYING LASAGNA.
END

WATCH OUT FOR
PAPERCUTZ ™

Welcome to the second GARFIELD & Co graphic novel from Papercutz, the graphic novel publisher dedicated to producing great graphic novels for all ages. I'm Jim Salicrup, the Editor-in-Chief at Papercutz, and Assistant Lasagna Chef. In our first GARFIELD & Co graphic novel I told you all about the creator of Garfield, the one and only Jim Davis. This time around I'd like to tell you a little bit about Papercutz...

Launched way back in 2005 by publisher Terry Nantier and me, editor Jim Salicrup, Papercutz started off with the graphic novel debuts of THE HARDY BOYS and NANCY DREW. Recently, we relaunched both series in larger-sized formats. If you're lucky, you can still find copies available at your favorite bookseller—be they a comicbook store, bookstore, or online store—of the first two volumes of NANCY DREW The New Case Files and THE HARDY BOYS The New Case Files. The world-famous Girl Detective runs into someone her friends believe is a blood-sucking monster, who happens to be hot, in the two-part "Vampire Slayer" saga, while the Undercover Brothers also seem to face supernatural forces in "Crawling with Zombies."

Some of Papercutz's recent best-sellers include TALES FROM THE CRYPT-- the 8th and 9th volumes featuring "Diary of a Stinky Dead Kid," a twisted parody of another best-selling kids series we suspect you might be familiar with.

While the Papercutz version of TALES FROM THE CRYPT now features horrific parodies, we recently launched PAPERCUTZ SLICES which also features pun-filled parodies of various pop culture phenomena. The first volume featured "Harry Potty and the Deathly Boring," while the second shined the spotlight on "breaking down," a spoof of a certain series of sappy vampire novels and movies. Coming up next in PAPERCUTZ SLICES: "Percy Jerkson & the Ovolactovegetarians."

We also publish another graphic novel series that features an orange cat and his rather odd master. The orange cat is Azrael and his master is a wizard called Gargamel, and the two of them spend way too much time causing trouble for THE SMURFS. You may have heard that there's a big 3D movie starring the SMURFS coming to theaters everywhere this summer, but did you know THE SMURFS actually started out as comicbook characters? It's true. THE SMURFS, created by Peyo, first appeared in 1958, and it wasn't until the 80s that they came to the USA in their hit, long-running animated TV series. To see what all the excitement is about, just check out THE SMURFS graphic novels—each one is packed with adventure, fun, and lots of Smurfs!

There's another super-successful series that we publish, but we're a little afraid to talk about it here in GARFIELD & Co. You see, it's called GERONIMO STILTON, and it features the adventures of a time-travelling newspaper editor and his friends and family. If you're already familiar with GERONIMO STILTON from his many best-selling books, then you know why I'm a little nervous mentioning Geronimo here. If you're not already a GERONIMO STILTON fan, may I suggest checking out his series of graphic novels from Papercutz? As soon as you see it, you'll know why I'm being a little skittish, and haven't mentioned the M-word.

Uh-oh! I just barely have enough room to mention that coming soon to booksellers everywhere: GARFIELD & Co #3 "Catzilla" -- with three more exciting episodes of our favorite work-adverse feline. Don't miss it!

Till then, watch out for Papercutz!

Jim

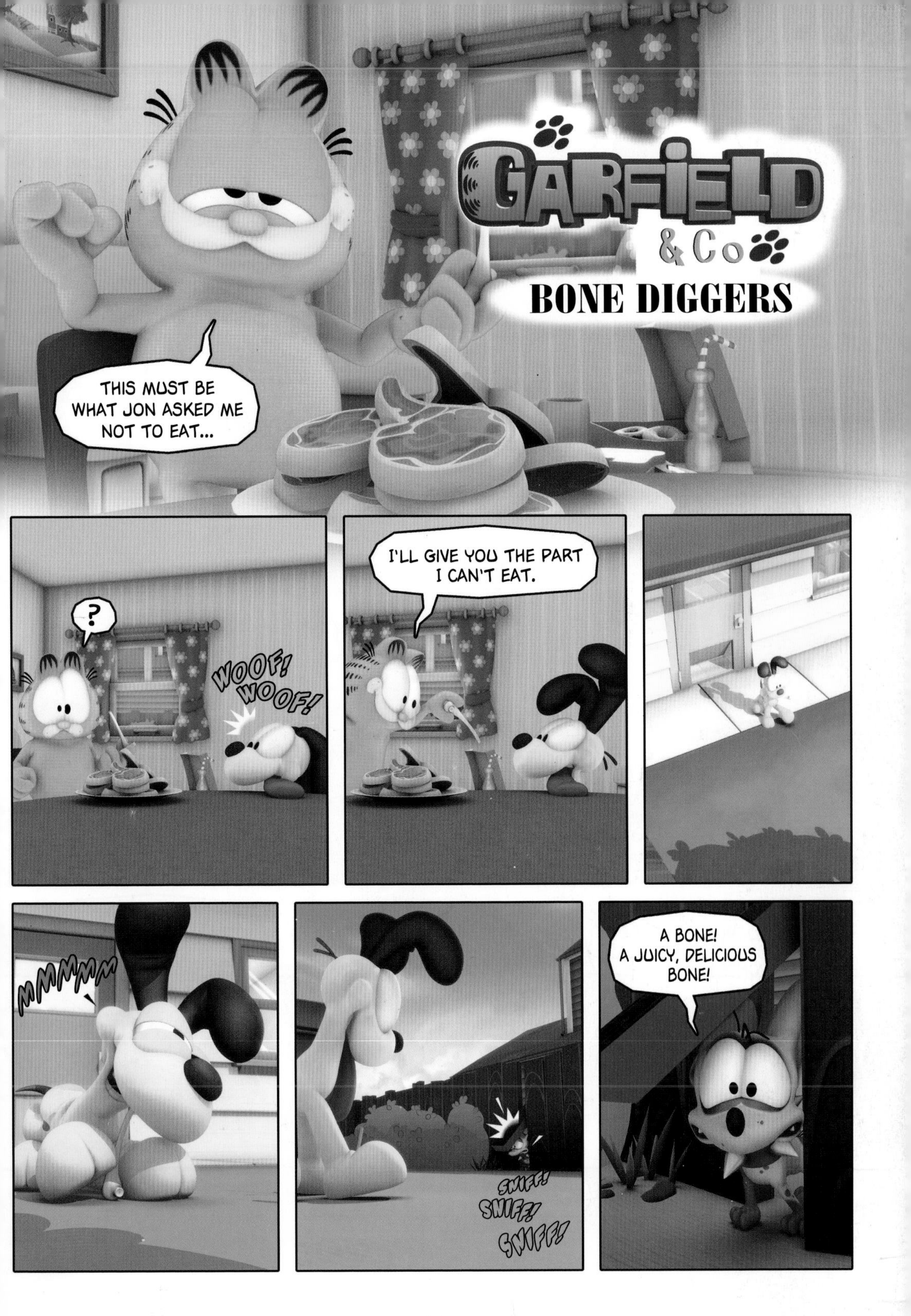
GARFIELD
& Co
BONE DIGGERS
THIS MUST BE WHAT JON ASKED ME NOT TO EAT...
?
WOOF! WOOF!
I'LL GIVE YOU THE PART I CAN'T EAT.
MMMMM
SNIFF! SNIFF! SNIFF!
A BONE! A JUICY, DELICIOUS BONE!

HEY, ODIE! LOOK AT THAT MOCKINGBIRD!

?

JUMP

HA HA HA! THAT MOCKINGBIRD IS MOCKING YOU!

YOU WANT ANOTHER BONE?

YOU FINISHED THE LAST ONE? IF YOU WANT A BONE, GO DIG UP ONE OF THOSE YOU'VE BURIED IN THE GARDEN.

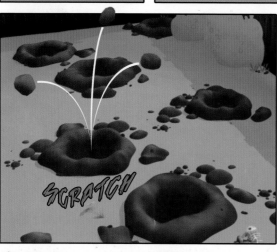

SCRATCH

SNIFF

SO, YOU'VE FOUND A BIG BONE. BIG DEAL. DON'T BOTHER ME.

WOOF! WOOF!

IF IT ONLY HAD MEAT ON IT! WAIT! DO YOU KNOW WHAT THAT IS, ODIE?

COME AND SEE!

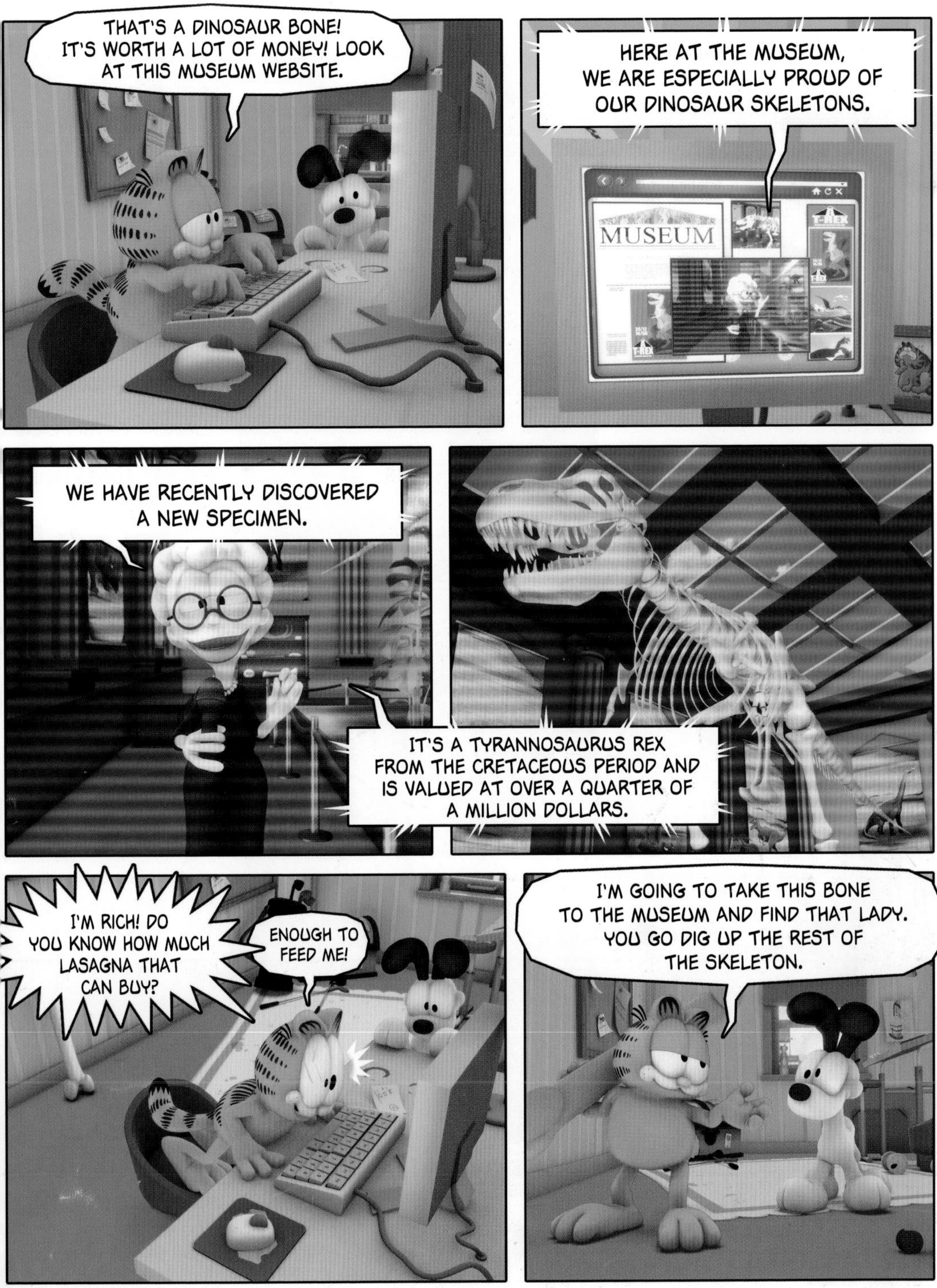
THAT'S A DINOSAUR BONE! IT'S WORTH A LOT OF MONEY! LOOK AT THIS MUSEUM WEBSITE.
HERE AT THE MUSEUM, WE ARE ESPECIALLY PROUD OF OUR DINOSAUR SKELETONS.
MUSEUM
T-REX
WE HAVE RECENTLY DISCOVERED A NEW SPECIMEN.
IT'S A TYRANNOSAURUS REX FROM THE CRETACEOUS PERIOD AND IS VALUED AT OVER A QUARTER OF A MILLION DOLLARS.
I'M RICH! DO YOU KNOW HOW MUCH LASAGNA THAT CAN BUY?
ENOUGH TO FEED ME!
I'M GOING TO TAKE THIS BONE TO THE MUSEUM AND FIND THAT LADY. YOU GO DIG UP THE REST OF THE SKELETON.

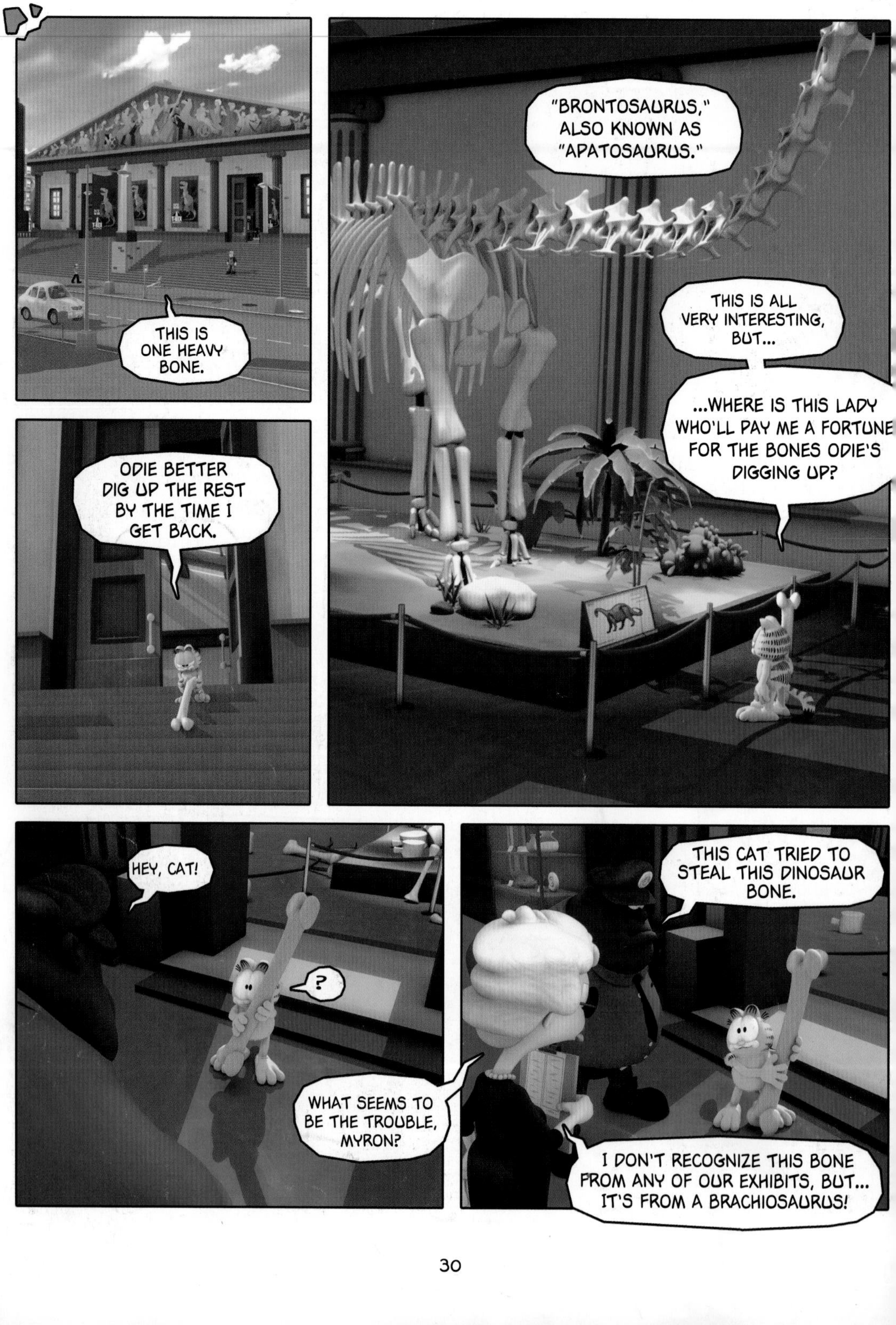
THIS IS ONE HEAVY BONE.
ODIE BETTER DIG UP THE REST BY THE TIME I GET BACK.
"BRONTOSAURUS," ALSO KNOWN AS "APATOSAURUS."
THIS IS ALL VERY INTERESTING, BUT...
...WHERE IS THIS LADY WHO'LL PAY ME A FORTUNE FOR THE BONES ODIE'S DIGGING UP?
HEY, CAT!
?
WHAT SEEMS TO BE THE TROUBLE, MYRON?
THIS CAT TRIED TO STEAL THIS DINOSAUR BONE.
I DON'T RECOGNIZE THIS BONE FROM ANY OF OUR EXHIBITS, BUT... IT'S FROM A BRACHIOSAURUS!

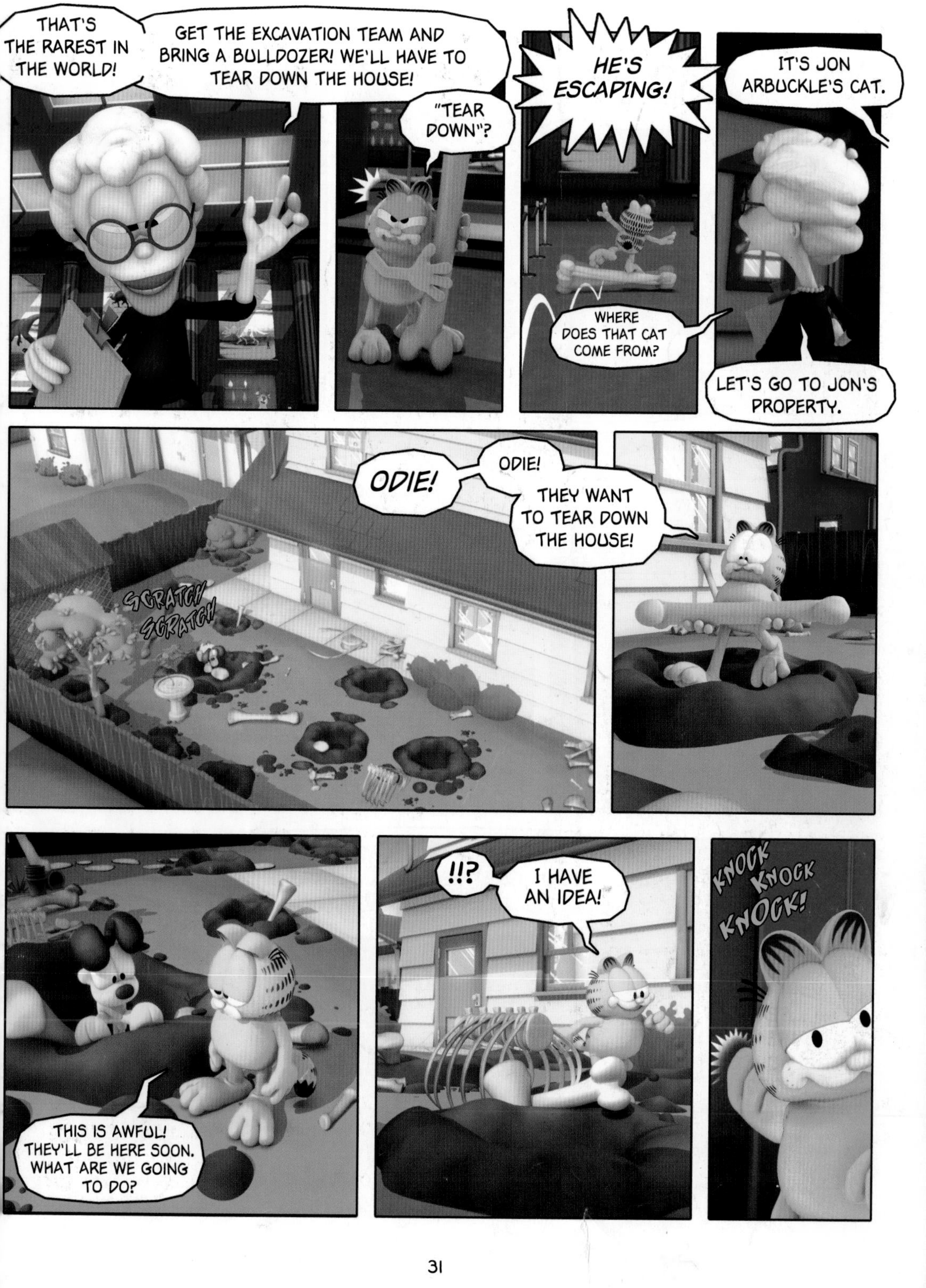
THAT'S THE RAREST IN THE WORLD!
GET THE EXCAVATION TEAM AND BRING A BULLDOZER! WE'LL HAVE TO TEAR DOWN THE HOUSE!
"TEAR DOWN"?
HE'S ESCAPING!
WHERE DOES THAT CAT COME FROM?
IT'S JON ARBUCKLE'S CAT.
LET'S GO TO JON'S PROPERTY.
SCRATCH SCRATCH
ODIE!
ODIE!
THEY WANT TO TEAR DOWN THE HOUSE!
THIS IS AWFUL! THEY'LL BE HERE SOON. WHAT ARE WE GOING TO DO?
!!?
I HAVE AN IDEA!
KNOCK KNOCK KNOCK!

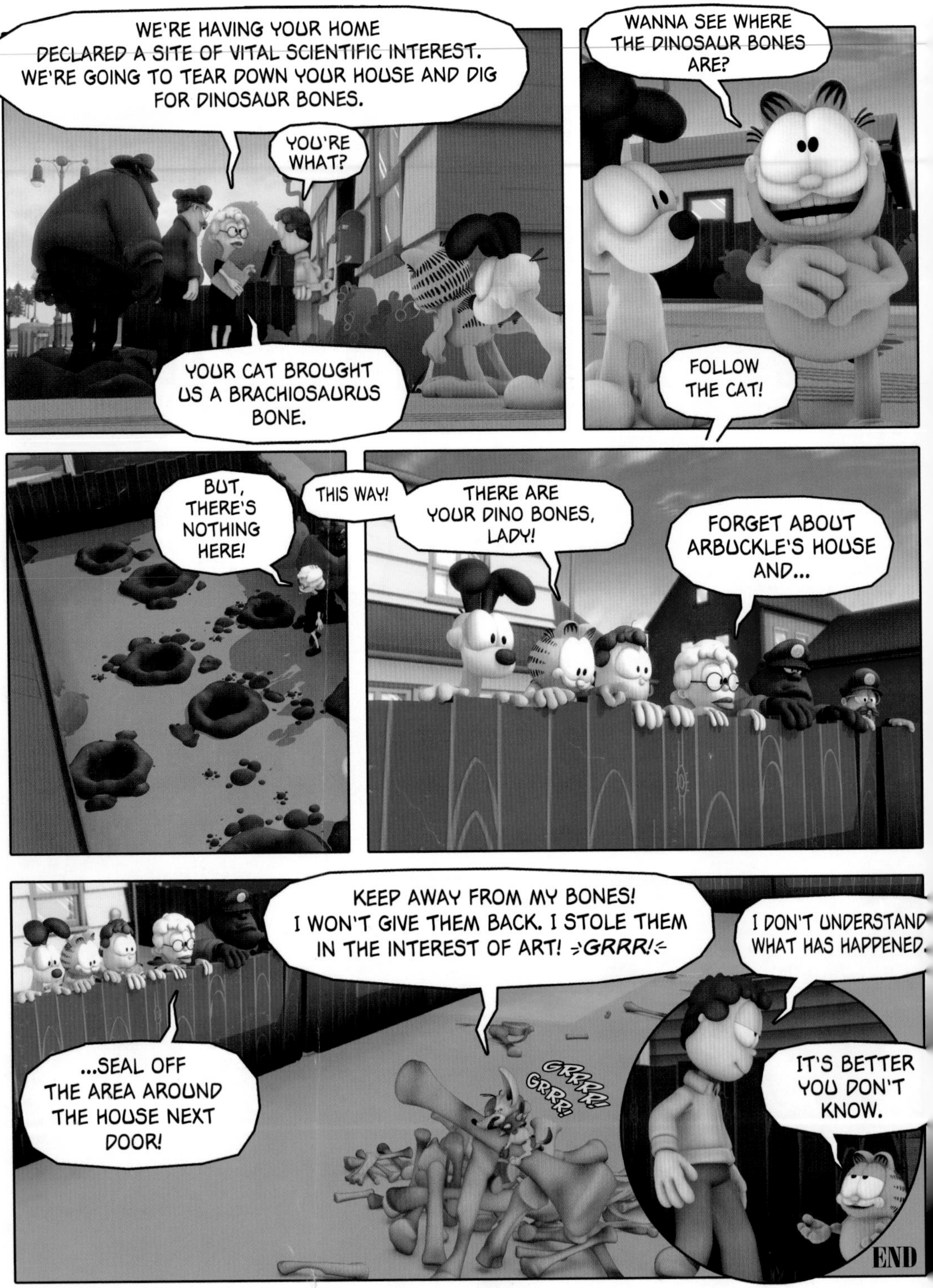
WE'RE HAVING YOUR HOME DECLARED A SITE OF VITAL SCIENTIFIC INTEREST. WE'RE GOING TO TEAR DOWN YOUR HOUSE AND DIG FOR DINOSAUR BONES.
YOU'RE WHAT?
YOUR CAT BROUGHT US A BRACHIOSAURUS BONE.
WANNA SEE WHERE THE DINOSAUR BONES ARE?
FOLLOW THE CAT!
BUT, THERE'S NOTHING HERE!
THIS WAY!
THERE ARE YOUR DINO BONES, LADY!
FORGET ABOUT ARBUCKLE'S HOUSE AND...
...SEAL OFF THE AREA AROUND THE HOUSE NEXT DOOR!
KEEP AWAY FROM MY BONES! I WON'T GIVE THEM BACK. I STOLE THEM IN THE INTEREST OF ART! GRRR!
GRRR! GRRR!
I DON'T UNDERSTAND WHAT HAS HAPPENED.
IT'S BETTER YOU DON'T KNOW.
END